RUN AGROUND

LANTERN BEACH MAYDAY, BOOK 1

CHRISTY BARRITT

River Heights

CHAPTER ONE

MACKENZIE ANDERSON STEPPED from her car, closed her eyes, and inhaled the scent of salty water and fish.

And hope.

At least, if hope had a scent, this was what it would smell like.

She opened her eyes again and stared at the harbor in front of her. The weather-worn waterfront was so unlike the clean, manicured marinas she'd grown up around.

This was a workingman's harbor, filled with mostly fishing vessels and workers who looked as weathered as the wooden docks.

Except for the 120-foot yacht in the distance.

That vessel would be her home for the next eight weeks.

Kenzie—as friends called her—was really doing this. Despite her father's wishes. Despite the advanced education waiting for her back home. Despite everything.

She needed to take this job for herself.

Just for a season.

Maybe.

As people liked to say, she needed to find herself. Or maybe she just needed breathing room. She wasn't sure the exact motivation for the urging inside her.

Either way, she was about to embark on the journey of a lifetime.

Pulling her rolling suitcase behind her, she started toward the dock. Captain Larry Bridgemore should be meeting her aboard *Almost Paradise*.

She didn't have a lot of maritime experience. She'd worked on her uncle's sailboat a couple of weeks each summer in high school, then she'd worked one summer—before med school started— on a smaller yacht based out of Miami.

But Kenzie knew she could do this. She'd taken the STCW—the Standards of Training, Certification, and Watchkeeping, a course that sets qualifications for personnel on seagoing ships—as well as stewardess training. The classes had used up almost all her money, but she prayed the sacrifice would be worth it.

The sunlight flooding her shoulders seemed to promise that.

Her flip-flops flapped across the gravel lot as she hurried toward the superyacht. She was a little early, but she hoped the captain would see that as an asset.

She'd interviewed for the job via a video call, so she'd never met the man face-to-face. He'd seemed nice enough, if not a little loud and gruff. Still, getting away from everyday life for weeks at a time on this boat would be an answer to prayer.

Kenzie pushed down her nerves as she reached the boat slip.

She left her sensible gray suitcase there, figuring it was best not to climb aboard with it now.

But, as she stared at the wooden dock leading to the boat, her throat tightened.

Small dark-red specks formed a jagged line leading to the gangplank.

Was that . . . ?

Kenzie shook her head.

Not blood.

Not human blood, at least.

Maybe it was some type of liquid from a fishing trip. That made the most sense, right? But Kenzie knew nothing about fishing. That was just a guess.

Still, her lungs felt tight as she continued toward the yacht. The spots of blood became bigger with every step.

Part of her wanted to turn back. To run. To agree with her dad that this was a terrible idea.

But she'd come this far, and she didn't want to overreact.

Stuffing down her fears, she removed her shoes —as per the barefoot policy to avoid damaging the yacht's luxurious teakwood—and stepped onto the gangplank.

Her steps slowed as she boarded the boat. "Hello? Anybody here?"

She was thirty minutes early, but the rest of the crew should be here soon. They had to get the boat ready to depart tomorrow. That was when their guests would arrive, anticipating being pampered as they embarked on the adventure of a lifetime.

She called again, "Hello? Is anyone there?"

When only silence answered, she stepped farther onto the boat. Perhaps the captain was on the bridge. That made the most sense.

Kenzie would try once more, and if she still

couldn't find Captain Bridgemore, she'd head back to the dock and wait until their meeting time.

Her gaze went to the deck, and she sucked in a breath.

More red droplets.

What was going on?

She reached for the door and pulled it open. Before she could call for the captain again, her lungs froze.

A man lay on the floor in front of her, blood covering the chest of his white uniform.

A blood-curdling scream escaped from her lungs as her head began to spin.

It was Captain Bridgemore.

JIMMY JAMES GAMBLE heard the scream from across the harbor. He dropped the water hose he'd been using to clean the twenty-eight-foot Valentino that had just come in from a fishing charter.

He hoped the scream hadn't come from the woman with the expensive suitcase he'd seen walking toward the luxury yacht that had arrived in the harbor yesterday.

But he had a feeling that was exactly where the sound had come from.

As he ran across the boardwalk, he quickly scanned the area.

That's when he saw the pretty brunette backing out from the interior of *Almost Paradise*.

She nearly stumbled over the edge of the boat, but she caught herself on the gangplank railing.

Her pale skin and trembling limbs clearly showed distress.

Jimmy James started down the dock but froze. He glanced at the wood planks beneath him.

Was that . . . blood?

Did it belong to the woman in front of him?

He didn't think so, but caution stretched taut across his muscles.

Something was seriously wrong.

He hurried up the gangplank and paused beside the woman.

"Are you okay?" He gripped her arms and looked for signs she'd been injured. He saw none.

Her expression remained slack as she stared inside the salon.

Jimmy James followed her gaze and sucked in a breath.

The captain . . . lay dead on the floor.

Blood stained the chest of his uniform.

Gunshot wound or knife?

Jimmy James didn't know.

Right now, all he knew was that he needed to call the police.

He took the woman's arm and tugged her away from the body. She didn't need to see any more than she already had.

He dialed 911 and reported the death then turned back to the woman in front of him.

His main concern was making sure she didn't pass out and that they didn't have another casualty as she toppled into the water.

As he slipped his phone back into his pocket, he turned to her. "What's your name?"

"Mackenzie . . ." Her words sounded dull, and her eyes still looked glazed. "Mackenzie Anderson, but my friends call me Kenzie."

"Kenzie, my name is Jimmy James. The police are on the way. It's going to be okay, understand?"

She nodded, even though he wasn't at all confident that she truly understood. She still seemed stunned.

He quickly glanced around.

No one else was nearby.

Most of the charter fishing vessels were still out,

except for a few half days that were already back. Jimmy James was taking care of several of the boats that remained docked. Mostly fishing vessels operated out of this marina. But about a month ago, he'd heard about a luxury yacht owner that wanted to operate charters out of Lantern Beach.

The decision didn't make sense to him. Lantern Beach, North Carolina, was no Fort Lauderdale. But the boat's owner seemed determined to make a go of it.

An image of the dead captain filled his mind again. Jimmy James had just met the man yesterday.

Captain Larry Bridgemore had come across as curt, loud, and boisterous—the type who liked to make his presence known. He'd been bragging to anyone who'd listen about how much money he and his crew would be bringing in doing these luxury charters.

Right now, Jimmy James needed to concentrate on helping the woman in front of him. "Where are you from, Kenzie?"

"Delaware," she muttered. Her pupils looked large, and her breathing sounded fast—classic signs of shock.

"What brings you to Lantern Beach? Let me guess, you're a guest on the charter?"

She pointed to herself. "Me? No."

"You're a marine biology student here for a summer program to study tidal tributaries along the island?"

Her startled gaze met his, and she stared at him a moment before shaking her head. "Wrong again. I'm actually going to be working as a steward on *Almost Paradise*."

He sucked in a breath at her pronouncement. He hadn't pegged the woman for a crew member. She seemed too refined. Reserved. Cultured. Then again, what did he know?

Jimmy James was just a dockhand himself—someone who'd barely gotten his life back together over the past five years.

He was trying to do better. Every day he woke up with that goal in mind. Most days he succeeded, but he'd had a few setbacks.

"Listen." He leaned down to make eye contact with the woman, who was a good foot shorter than he was. "Let's get you off this boat and find you some water to drink. The police should be here anytime now, and they'll take over the scene. They'll have some questions to ask you."

Even though he'd been the one to call the police, past experience caused his spine to tighten.

For most of his life, Jimmy James had been on the wrong side of the law.

But he hadn't been in trouble in a long time. Besides, he trusted the police chief here on the island. She was a good woman—a fair woman.

Kenzie nodded and slipped her shoes back on. Then Jimmy James led her from the boat to the dock, careful to avoid the splotches of blood beneath them.

Just as they reached the parking area, two police vehicles arrived on the scene.

Hopefully, Cassidy and her officers would be able to sort this all out.

But Jimmy James was certain this was no accident.

Someone had murdered Captain Bridgemore.

CHAPTER TWO

KENZIE COULDN'T GET the image of Captain Bridgemore's lifeless body out of her mind. Even as she stood in the gravel parking lot, every time she closed her eyes, all she saw was the harsh red blood splotch against his crisp white uniform.

The stranger who'd helped her stood beside her now.

At any other time, Kenzie would have probably feared the man.

Jimmy James was big. Muscular. Tall. Had more tattoos than she could politely count. His dark hair was shaved close to his skin, his square face had a hint of stubble, and his brownish-green eyes looked like he'd seen and experienced far more than Kenzie wanted to imagine.

In a brutish way, he was handsome and tough.

Yet he didn't look like someone Kenzie would want to run into alone in a dark alley.

However, he'd been nothing but kind as he helped her through this situation, and he'd stayed by her side while the police checked out the boat.

Even now, as the police chief took Kenzie's statement, he remained close, prompting Kenzie whenever her thoughts drifted back to her horrific discovery.

"Is this your first time meeting Captain Bridgemore?" the police chief asked.

Kenzie turned back to the woman. Chief Chambers was probably in her early thirties, with blonde hair that had been pulled back into a bun and a growing belly. She definitely looked pregnant—but Kenzie knew better than to ask. The woman's intelligent eyes were prodding but kind, firm yet compassionate.

Kenzie sucked in a deep breath before pushing her hair back from her face. "I never met Captain Bridgemore in person. We only talked through an online video chat when I interviewed for the job. It's the only reason I even knew what he looked like."

"I see."

She pressed her lips together, holding back the

cry that wanted to escape. "I wish there was more that I could tell you, but I just came over on the ferry this morning. I haven't met anyone else on the island yet or even on the crew, for that matter."

"I understand." Chief Chambers jotted something else on her notepad. "I'm sorry you had to see that. Is there anything else that I can get for you? Another water?"

She'd sent one of her officers to get a bottle earlier. Kenzie must have looked like she could pass out.

"No, I think I'll be fine." Kenzie rubbed her head as she felt an ache forming at her temples. The sun beat down on her, causing sweat to trickle across her skin. Seagulls squawked overhead. Normally, the sound would be comforting. Right now, they almost sounded taunting.

What a nightmare. Not only that, but she had to figure out where to go from here. Her father wasn't speaking to her. She wouldn't be welcomed back at home, not after that last conversation with her stepmom. She had no Plan B.

She was going to have to figure something out. She only had two hundred dollars in her checking account right now, and that amount wouldn't get her very far.

Chief Chambers turned to the man beside her. He'd been lingering close, although she wasn't sure if that was because he anticipated being questioned or if he wanted to catch Kenzie in case she collapsed.

"Jimmy James, have you ever seen the captain before?" the police chief asked.

"I have." Jimmy James' jaw stiffened. "Just last night. I met him briefly, and he told me about this new charter. Seemed pretty excited."

Chief Chambers rubbed her belly before letting out a breath. "I understand. Have you seen anything suspicious here at the docks?"

Kenzie listened closely, noting the good rapport between this man and the police chief. Her curiosity grew as she wondered what their story was. He didn't seem like the clean-cut type of guy who'd be chummy with the police—more like the informant type.

Jimmy James shook his head. "Everything seemed pretty normal this morning. A bunch of tourists went out charter fishing. But I didn't see anything out of the ordinary. Was he shot?"

Chief Chambers shook her head and frowned. "By all appearances, the captain was stabbed."

"Did you find the murder weapon?"

She shifted, narrowing her eyes even more. "You

know I can't share very many details. But, no, we haven't found it yet. My guess is that someone threw it in the water. Around here, it's the easiest way to dispose of a weapon."

Kenzie shivered as she listened. It sounded so calculated when the chief said it that way.

Out of habit, she reached for the diamond stud in her ear and began to twirl it around.

Before Jimmy James could offer anything else, a car pulled into the lot. Two men and a woman climbed out and strode toward them. They each wore sunglasses, had tans, and their shorts and T-shirts looked too clean and pressed for them to be part of any fishing charters.

Their steps slowed when they saw the cops.

"What's going on here?" The taller man of the group heaved his bookbag over his shoulder, his gaze sliding from Chief Chambers to Jimmy James to Kenzie then back to the police chief again. "Is everything okay?"

"I'm Lantern Beach Police Chief Chambers. Who are you?"

"I'm Eddie, bosun for *Almost Paradise*."

Eddie was not only tall, but he was markedly thin. His hair was cut short, like a sailor's might be, and he had big blue eyes, a craggy nose, and sun-kissed skin marred with tan lines around his expensive sunglasses.

"These are my other crew members—Deckhand Owen Hemlock and Chief Steward Sunni Briggs," Eddie continued.

Sunni had a sturdy built, a heart-shaped face, and honey-blonde hair. But her eyes looked calculated, as if she liked to size people up.

Owen's height probably matched Kenzie's—somewhere around five foot seven. He had curly, light-brown hair, and his demeanor made him appear quiet and reserved.

"Eddie, I'm going to need to ask you and your crew members some questions." The chief glanced at each of them and waited for them to nod. Her voice sounded no-nonsense, as if she dared anyone to question her.

"Questions about what?" Eddie asked.

"Unfortunately, your captain was found dead earlier."

Gasps went around the group.

"What happened?" Sunni asked. "How can he be dead?"

Kenzie took the last sip of her water and rubbed her temples one more time.

Her thoughts continued to race as she tried to

figure out exactly how she was going to get through this situation. She thought she'd hit rock bottom before.

Apparently, she still had farther to fall.

JIMMY JAMES WATCHED as shock rolled over the features of the three crew members who'd just shown up.

They all looked as he'd expected. On the younger side. Out for adventure. In disbelief over the turn of events.

No doubt, they were each trying to process and recalculate.

Beside him, he sensed the tremor that raced through Kenzie.

He wasn't sure why he felt protective of the woman. They'd just met each other. But something about her seemed vulnerable and maybe even a touch naive. Everyone else felt like piranhas with their unfriendly demeanor and the way they cut their gazes at each other, silently communicating as if they knew something the rest of them didn't.

But, even more than that, why had Captain Bridgemore been stabbed and killed? Had he found himself in the middle of a situation he wasn't supposed to be a part of? Did this somehow tie into the upcoming charter cruise?

"I'm going to call Mr. Robertson." Bosun Eddie pulled out his cell phone. "He needs to know what's going on."

"Who is Mr. Robertson?" Chief Chambers eyed him suspiciously.

"He owns *Almost Paradise*. Even though Captain Bridgemore usually calls the shots, I answer to the Robertsons. Bill is going to want to know what happened, especially since we have guests coming in tomorrow, expecting to take the yacht out on a four-day excursion. Do you think the boat will be cleared by then?"

Chief Chambers shrugged, her expression unreadable. "I'll do everything I can, but right now the boat is a crime scene, and you have no captain."

Eddie scowled, not necessarily at Cassidy but at the situation. "So, what am I supposed to tell him?"

"Would you like me to talk to him?"

Eddie stared at her a moment, an unreadable emotion in his eyes, before he finally shook his head. "Nah, I've got this. He should hear it from me first."

Jimmy James listened as the man chatted with the boat's owner.

Eddie ended the call a few minutes later and turned to address everyone. "Does anybody know where we can find a new captain?"

Kenzie sucked in a breath beside him before murmuring, "You mean this charter is still going out?"

"This is our livelihood," Eddie explained. "If this charter cruise doesn't happen, we're all out of a job. The Morenos are already on their way here, coming from Raleigh. We need to do everything we can to accommodate them."

Everyone's gaze turned back to Cassidy.

Her toughness faded for just a moment as she fanned her face and rubbed her back.

Pregnancy discomfort, Jimmy James assumed. It was warm outside for the July day, and the humidity certainly couldn't help.

"I'm not going to promise anything," she finally said, her voice firm and unwavering. "We'll do our best to work this crime scene, and then I'll let you know. But this boat isn't going anywhere if you don't have a captain."

"Where are we going to find a captain at such late notice?" Owen asked as he turned to Eddie.

"The Robertsons probably have some connections, but I really don't know." Eddie shrugged. "It's not looking good, is it?"

Jimmy James wasn't sure what came over him, but he found himself stepping forward and announcing, "I can do it."

Everyone stared at him in surprise.

"You have your captain's license?" Chief Chambers sounded shocked, as if she hadn't heard him correctly.

He nodded slowly. He'd been hesitant to share that news with everyone, and now he realized it must seem out of the blue.

"I do. I've been working on it for a while now. I did the sixty-hour course. Got certified in CPR. Got my hours in. Jumped through all the hoops. I'm qualified, and I can show you the paperwork to prove it."

"How many people are you approved to take?" Eddie narrowed his eyes suspiciously.

"Twelve."

Eddie pushed his Oakley sunglasses up higher on his nose and nodded slowly as if processing the update. "Do you have availability?"

"If I had a serious offer, I could probably make it happen." Jimmy James shrugged. Even though he was supposed to be working as a dockhand, this seemed more important.

Especially since he had no idea what kind of trouble was lingering beneath the surface of this whole operation.

His decision had nothing to do with Kenzie. That's what Jimmy James told himself. Still, the woman stirred all his protective instincts.

Kind of like Lucy had—and he'd failed Lucy. He'd vowed he wouldn't let that happen again.

Eddie continued to scrutinize him with narrowed eyes and lips pressed into a tight line. "Let me call Mr. Robertson back and see what he says."

Jimmy James nodded. He wasn't sure exactly what he might be getting himself into.

But his gut told him he couldn't let this go.

If there was one thing a life of crime had taught him, it was to sense trouble the moment it came close.

And his senses were waving red flags right now.

CHAPTER THREE

KENZIE CURLED on the bed of the little inn where she was staying for the night. She only managed to get a room because someone had canceled at the last minute. Almost all the properties here on the island were apparently booked solid this time of year.

The rest of the crew had found a site at a nearby campground and hadn't offered to let Kenzie stay with them. What a great start to this new chapter in her life.

She pressed her head into the cotton-scented pillow, trying to calm her anxious heart. Every time she closed her eyes, she pictured Captain Bridgemore's dead body. Fear tried to swallow her—fear because whoever had done that to the captain was still out there somewhere. Though she had no reason to believe she would be targeted, she still felt uneasy.

She let out a breath, trying to get her racing heart under control.

The good news was that more crew members were coming tomorrow. Maybe they'd be a little more friendly than the three she'd met today. Unfortunately, the boat's owner had found another captain to use instead of Jimmy James. Kenzie had really been hoping he might get the position.

Even with another captain lined up, Kenzie tried to block out the "what ifs" that only increased her anxiety. If this job fell through . . . she didn't know what she would do. She had an undergraduate degree in biology, and she was sure she could find something in that field. But it wouldn't be a job she necessarily wanted to do.

Worries swept through her mind like a hurricane destroying everything in its path. She could hear her stepmother's voice in her head right now, telling her, "I told you so."

Her dad *definitely* hadn't supported her coming here, and in some ways, Kenzie couldn't blame him. Her father had charted the course of her future, and she'd simply realized too late that his plans didn't match the direction of her heart. She only wished things hadn't turned out the way they did . . .

She sighed and glanced at the red numbers on the alarm clock sitting on the nightstand. It was already ten o'clock. She should really get some sleep because tomorrow could end up being a long day.

She reached for her earrings to take them off.

One of them was missing.

A fresh round of panic rushed through her. What happened to it?

She searched her memories for any occasion it might have slipped off. When was the last time she remembered having it on?

That was right. Kenzie had been standing in the gravel parking lot near the harbor and, as the police chief had questioned her, she'd twirled the diamond stud.

What if it fell out then?

The jewelry had been her mom's, and the thought of the stud lying where someone else might find it caused a swell of sadness inside her.

She had to go back to the harbor and see if she could locate it. She was on a sleepy little island. Certainly, she'd be fine going out at night alone. It wasn't like she was in the big city where crime was around every corner.

So why did she still feel a stab of fear?

She pushed the feeling down. Instead, she rose from bed, pulled on a sweatshirt, and slipped on her shoes. She grabbed her things and went to her car to drive to the harbor.

As she remembered Captain Bridgemore's dead body, she hoped she didn't regret this choice. A shiver raced down her spine at the possibility.

JIMMY JAMES STOOD in the shadows near the marina office and watched the boats bobbing on the water at the docks. He relished the moment of peace as a sliver of moonlight barely illuminated the harbor.

Normally, he'd head to the little bungalow he called home after his shift was over. But, after what had happened earlier, he'd decided to stick around a little longer.

Besides, the harbormaster was a good friend, and Jimmy James wanted to make sure no one started more trouble here. These docks felt like his territory, his domain. He was protective of the space, and he didn't like it when people tried to disturb the peace here.

The harbor was usually quiet at night. During the day, it was bustling at times as fishermen came and went. As they bragged about what they'd caught and compared the day's bounties to see who had the biggest catch.

But at night everything seemed to settle down.

Except over the past couple of weeks.

He'd noticed a few new people hanging out in the area recently. Initially, he'd dismissed the newcomers. Jimmy James figured they were just some college kids out for trouble, and that it wasn't any of his business.

But the fact that Captain Bridgemore had been found dead today changed his perspective.

He hadn't mentioned the guys to Cassidy. He *almost* had. But he hadn't seen them around last night, and he didn't want to throw anyone under the bus.

As he lingered in the shadows, his mind drifted back to the events of today. He thought about meeting Kenzie. The woman just seemed so out of place here. Why had she come? Why had she taken this job?

He didn't know, but he was curious. A rush of concern filled him when he pictured her being on

Almost Paradise. Out in the middle of the ocean. With no one to watch out for her.

If he were honest with himself, Jimmy James would admit that part of the reason he'd volunteered to be captain was because Kenzie would be on the boat—which seemed crazy since he didn't even know her.

But it was the truth.

Nonetheless, the position hadn't worked out. He just hoped the woman would be okay.

As Kenzie continued to occupy his thoughts, headlights in the distance caught his eye. A car pulled into the harbor area and parked at the back of the lot. A moment later, someone climbed out and the beam of a flashlight hit the ground.

Jimmy James tried to get a better look, but the darkness of the night made it hard to see. The newcomer didn't appear to be one of the troublemakers he'd spotted earlier. This was only one person and . . . appeared to be a woman.

His back straightened. Wait . . . was that . . . Kenzie? What was she doing here? And what was with the flashlight and her hunched stance?

He remained where he was, watching, not wanting to scare her.

But his spine tightened when he heard voices on

the other side of the marina. He glanced in the direction of the sound and saw three guys talking near one of the boats.

This was the group he'd been concerned about. The new people who'd been hanging out down at the docks. He thought they could be up to trouble.

He glanced back at the woman he assumed was Kenzie and noticed she didn't even raise her head at the sound of the voices or glance at her surroundings.

Then he peered back at the three figures talking behind him. The light from Kenzie's flashlight caught their attention, and they quieted. The next instant, they murmured something to each other before letting out long, drawn-out chuckles.

Suggestive chuckles.

Jimmy James' chest tightened. He knew what that meant.

He knew there was about to be trouble.

CHAPTER FOUR

KENZIE LOOKED up as she heard footsteps. She froze when she saw three men striding toward her.

Fear spread through her veins like an arctic freeze. Who were these guys? Her instincts signaled they were trouble.

Coming to the harbor at night was clearly not a good idea. She'd been bent over, looking for an earring that might not even be here. In the dark. Alone.

Bad idea.

Her first instinct urged her to run back to her car.

But it was too late. These guys were too close.

Instead, she raised her flashlight and shone it in the faces of the three men approaching her. "Who are you?"

In an instant, the three of them surrounded her. She could hardly breathe as she wondered what might happen next. She didn't even want to think about those possibilities, yet she couldn't stop.

They could rob her. Beat her. Hurt her in more ways than one. In fact, what if these guys were the ones who'd killed the captain?

Her heart thumped harder at the thought.

"What are you doing out here, pretty thing?" The man in the center stepped closer.

Kenzie smelled alcohol on him. He was clearly drunk.

"I was just about to leave." She willed her voice not to tremble, but it did anyway. Would these men sense her weakness? Use that to their advantage?

"We're having a little party over on our boat," the guy on her left said. "Why don't you come join us?"

Kenzie stepped back. "No, I'm fine."

The third man reached for her arm. "Maybe we weren't asking."

Her heart pounded out of control. If they forced her into their boat . . .

She swallowed hard.

There wasn't even anyone who would notice she was missing right now. The crew would just think she'd left . . . It would be a few weeks before her disappearance would be reported. Her dad would simply think she was out to sea and not speaking with him.

As the man tugged her toward the water, another round of panic flooded her.

Would she end up like Captain Bridgemore?

AS SOON AS Jimmy James saw one of the thugs touch Kenzie, a jolt of white-hot anger flowed through him. That was *not* going to happen.

He stepped from the shadows and charged toward them.

"Hey!" he yelled.

The trio all froze and turned toward him.

He continued storming their way and growled, "Take your hands off her."

One of the guys—the one in the middle—stepped toward Jimmy James, waving his head back and forth with arrogance. "I don't think we invited you to our party."

"I'm pretty sure this woman said no."

"You shouldn't involve yourself with this." The same guy leered at Jimmy James, getting in his face.

"Leave her alone," he demanded.

"And if we don't?"

Jimmy James fisted his hands at his side. He didn't want to resort to fighting. But he would if he had to.

"You need to walk away." His words came out a hiss.

"We'll walk away." The punk in the middle looked back at Kenzie. "But only if she comes with us."

Something closely resembling fury spread through his veins like lava. "I'm telling you—walk away."

"Who do you think you are? The Hulk?" The group's leader stared at Jimmy James. "Are we not going to like you if we make you angry?"

The two guys flanking either side of him let out a chuckle. One still had his hand on Kenzie's arm, fueling Jimmy James' anger.

Jimmy James rubbed his fist as if preparing to fight. He hoped it would just be an empty threat. "Do you really want to test out that theory?"

Something about the way he said the words must have gotten through to the guys. Their fearless leader remained silent a moment before taking a step back. "You know what? This isn't worth it. But next time, don't get involved in our business. Come on, guys."

The guy lifted his hand in the air and motioned for his crew to follow.

Jimmy James remained in place as he watched them leave. It wasn't until they were back on the boat that he turned toward Kenzie and studied her face. The dim moonlight highlighted her brown hair and the oval shape of her face.

"Are you okay?" he asked quietly.

"Yes . . . thank you." Her teeth practically chattered until she swallowed hard, clearly shaken.

"If you don't mind me asking, what are you doing out here alone at night?" Was she up to something also? Because there had to be more to her story than she was letting on.

Jimmy James didn't want to think that Kenzie could somehow be involved with what had happened, but her actions were suspicious. She'd even been heading toward *Almost Paradise* when he spotted her.

Coincidence?

He hoped so.

She rubbed her arms as if chilled. "I lost an earring earlier. I didn't want to waste any time in finding it. It's . . . well, it's really important to me."

"Were you able to locate it?"

She shook her head. "I wasn't."

"Maybe you should try again when it's daylight. This place is usually safe, but the harbor isn't a place for you to be at night by yourself."

"I can see that." She looked in the direction of the men who'd boarded the other boat. "Who are they?"

His jaw stiffened as he followed her gaze. "I don't know. They've only been coming around over the past couple of weeks. I haven't seen them before that, but I've seen enough to know they're trouble."

She stared off in the distance and shook her head. "If you hadn't shown up when you did . . ."

Against his better instincts, he reached forward and squeezed her arm. "I'm glad you're okay. I think you should head to your car and go back to wherever you're staying."

She nodded quickly. "That's a good idea."

"I'll walk with you."

She didn't argue as they started across the lot. Silence sounded around them except for the occasional squawk of some nearby birds. Noises from the boat where those three guys disappeared occasionally filled the air—their raucous laughter making him hope they wouldn't cause any more trouble.

Finally, they paused beside her car, and Kenzie looked up at him with gratitude in her gaze. "Thank you again."

He wished he knew her better. Wished he could offer to drive her home and make sure she was safely inside wherever she was staying. But he didn't.

"You just get home safely, okay?" he finally said. "The earring can wait until tomorrow."

She nodded quickly before slipping inside.

But as she drove away, the bad feeling in Jimmy James' gut continued to grow stronger.

CHAPTER FIVE

KENZIE FELT JIMMY JAMES' eyes on her as she drove away from the harbor.

Going out tonight had been a bad idea. A *very* bad idea. Looking back, she couldn't stop asking herself what she'd been thinking.

If Jimmy James hadn't shown up when he did . . .

Another shudder went down her spine.

She gripped the wheel as she continued down the dark road. What she'd really wanted was to stay in her car, unmoving, and compose herself. But there would be no composing herself while Jimmy James watched her with that worried look in his eyes.

Who were those guys? Clearly, they were up to no good. Did they have something to do with

Captain Bridgemore's death? Based on the vibes they'd given, it seemed like a good guess.

Kenzie had gone through all this trouble tonight, and she still hadn't found her earring. But she supposed she had bigger worries right now. She was just thankful to be alive.

She glanced in the rearview mirror again as she pulled away from the harbor, unable to shake the spooked feeling haunting her.

Darkness hung around—the kind of dark she'd experienced only a few times in her life. Back in Delaware, streetlights had littered suburbia. Out here, there wasn't a streetlight in sight.

She shivered.

For a moment, she wished she could revert to her childhood. A childhood where she'd felt safe and secure with her mom and her dad.

Then she'd lost her mom, and her dad had eventually married Leesa.

At the thought of the woman, nausea roiled in her gut. Leesa was part of the reason there was so much friction between Kenzie and her father. Leesa had wanted to get rid of Kenzie. Had wanted to drive a wedge between Kenzie and her father so Leesa could have him all to herself.

It looked like she'd gotten her way.

Kenzie was twenty-five years old. An adult. She was going to pull through this and prove to everyone that she could get by on her own.

But whatever happened tomorrow would be pivotal to how her future played out.

———

THE OLD JIMMY JAMES would have stormed over to those guys' boat and given them a piece of his mind. Probably more than that if he were honest. But self-control was a virtue—a very important one that he was determined to master.

As he stood in the shadows by the office again, he stared at the 45-foot custom Carolina Sportfisher boat named *Relentless*. Anger simmered inside him.

How dare they treat Kenzie like that? Or any woman?

Even more so, what were those guys up to? They weren't hanging around here just for pleasure. He could feel it in his bones.

First thing in the morning, he'd mention this incident to Cassidy. She needed to know just in case these guys had anything to do with Captain Bridgemore's death.

If tonight was any indicator, Kenzie would be an

easy target on the upcoming charter. Not only that, but any superyacht flaunted wealth, which made them targets to modern-day pirates.

The thought made heaviness press into his chest.

He felt powerless to do anything about it.

He still couldn't make sense of why *Almost Paradise* had docked here. The boat probably cost thirty million dollars. Weekly charters cost close to a hundred thousand.

The large vessel looked out of place here next to the regular fishing boats.

Jimmy James wanted to be a captain one day. He figured he'd start with fishing charters and work his way up. Not to superyachts like that one. But something more than a fishing charter.

First, he had to save his money. Either that or find a management company who'd want to take him on.

The charter yacht world was small. Most people knew each other. Once your reputation was ruined, it was hard to bounce back.

For now, he would keep an eye on *Relentless*. Maybe he'd even creep closer and see if he could overhear anything.

Sleep was overrated anyway.

CHAPTER SIX

JUST AS SHE'D PROMISED, Kenzie went to meet the rest of the crew back at the docks at nine a.m. sharp. She'd grabbed a donut and coffee from a pastry shop in town before heading to the meeting.

As she drove to the harbor, she couldn't help but replay yesterday's events. Again, she shivered.

First, Captain Bridgemore's death. Then those thugs who'd cornered her at the harbor.

Things could have turned out so much differently last night, but she was grateful that they hadn't. She hoped she might run into Jimmy James again so she could thank him.

She wasn't sure what this day would hold, but today's events would determine her future. That was certain.

She put her car in Park at a gravel lot near the back of the parking lot. As she exited, she left her suitcase inside. She needed to figure out if this trip was still on before she grabbed it.

In the distance, she saw the other three crew members huddled near *Almost Paradise*.

"If it isn't Mackenzie Anderson." Eddie Gavin paused from whatever he was saying and turned to greet her as she approached. "I didn't realize who you were yesterday. Sorry about that."

"It's no problem." She should have introduced herself.

She glanced around at the rest of the crew. Two new members joined them, and she was quickly introduced.

Siv Olsen was the engineer and first mate. He was tall and pale with blond hair—a very Scandinavian look. From their brief interaction, she had the impression he was quiet and thoughtful.

Durango Herne would serve as chef. He had curly dark hair that fell around his face and a lean physique that reminded her of a surfer. But when he spoke, he had a subtle French accent. He'd said something about his mother being from Paris and his father being a cowboy in Arizona.

The rest of the crew clearly knew each other—

some better than others. That was going to make things interesting. If the charter happened, she would be the odd person out.

She stuffed her hands in the pockets of her khaki shorts. "Any updates?"

"Chief Chambers said she'd meet us out here," Eddie started. "But even if she clears this boat, I have some bad news."

Her spine tightened. "What's that?"

"The backup captain Mr. Robertson had lined up can't make it. He came down with the stomach flu. And without a captain . . ."

"What about Jimmy James?" Kenzie offered.

The rest of the crew glanced at each other. Kenzie knew what they were thinking. The man looked rough. Like the type that might even have a criminal record. But, still, there was something about him she liked.

Just as the thoughts went through her head, a footstep sounded behind her, and she turned. She sucked in a breath when she saw Jimmy James standing there in captain attire. The crisp white uniform cleaned him up quite a bit. But the sleeves were so tight on his bulging biceps that she had to look away for fear of staring and embarrassing herself.

"I just got the call." Jimmy James' gaze met each person in the semicircle. "Mr. Robertson looked over my qualifications and asked me if I'd be willing to captain the boat, at least for this first charter."

No one said anything for a moment until finally Eddie cleared his throat, his voice sounding incredulous as he said, "I'm surprised he didn't tell us."

"I literally just got off the phone with him about twenty minutes ago. He said he'd call you in a few, after he took his dog for a walk. Sounds like he loves his little puppy an awful lot."

Eddie practically rolled his eyes. "Yes, he does. Blinky is great."

"Blinky? You mean Rex?"

Eddie smirked.

That had been a test, hadn't it?

Jimmy James frowned as if he realized that. "This will all be for nothing if the boat isn't cleared by the police in time. The Morenos are supposed to be here at two and, even if the boat's cleared, we still have a lot of work to get it in shape."

Jimmy James held up some papers in his hands. "Mr. Robertson sent over information on the guests. As soon as we're clear, we'll review everything. I've already written a list of what needs to be done. I'll need to meet with the first mate and chief steward.

We're going to have a lot to put together if this works out."

Kenzie tried to hide her surprise. But she had to admit she was shocked at how much Jimmy James seemed to know about the job. Captaining a boat of this size wasn't something just anyone could do. It required extra training and experience.

But deep inside, she was rooting for Jimmy James.

She'd feel a lot better about going out to sea with someone like him at the helm.

JIMMY JAMES STEPPED BACK as the rest of the crew began to chat there on the docks.

He'd received a call from Mr. Robertson this morning, just as he'd told the crew. But even before that, he'd started to put together a to-do list just in case.

He hadn't gotten any sleep last night anyway, so it had worked out.

He'd remained at the harbor well into the night trying to keep an eye on the boat full of rabbler-ousers. Finally, at three a.m., they'd turned out their lights and apparently gone to sleep.

Jimmy James figured they wouldn't be into any more trouble—at least not for the time being.

But when he'd arrived back at the harbor this morning, he noticed that their boat was already gone. Had they taken it out for a joyride? To go fishing? To move on to another harbor?

He didn't know. With any luck, he wouldn't see them again.

Before the crew could question him anymore, Cassidy Chambers pulled up in her police SUV. Jimmy James hoped she would have an update.

A few minutes later, she strode toward them. Jimmy James tried to get a read on her body language, but he couldn't.

She paused at the edge of the circle. "Good morning. I see everyone's here and eager to get onboard."

"We're anxious to know what's going on." Eddie slid on his sunglasses.

Was that because the sun was bright or because he wanted to hide something from the police chief?

Jimmy James waited with bated breath to hear what she might say.

"I do have an update for you," Chief Chambers started. "Based on the evidence, we believe that Captain Bridgemore was killed as part of a robbery."

Gasps went around the circle.

"Why do you think that?" Sunni asked.

"His wallet and phone were missing," the chief explained. "Some charges were made on his credit cards in Fayetteville as well. We believe the captain fought this robber off on the dock and that resulted in him being stabbed. Most likely, he tried to get onboard for safety and to call for help. But by then it was too late."

"That's terrible." Eddie shook his head, his voice low with respect. "I'd only worked with Captain Bridgemore one other time, but he seemed like a good man."

Cassidy nodded somberly. "That said, we believe we've gotten all the evidence we need from the boat. I'm going to release the vessel back to the Robert-sons. I've already talked to them about it. If you're able to get things cleaned up in time, then you're free to take the boat out."

An almost audible sigh of relief went through the group.

Jimmy James was sure most of the people here were relying on the income they'd receive through this work to pay their bills for the summer. He couldn't fault them for that.

The crew began to talk amongst themselves as they seemed to process this new development.

As they did, Cassidy turned to him. "You're looking quite dapper."

"That's right. You can call me Captain now." Jimmy James flashed a grin as he smoothed his sleeves.

A smile tugged at her lips.

Most people in law enforcement were wary of people like Jimmy James. But Chief Chambers always seemed willing to give him a chance, and he greatly appreciated that.

His thoughts shifted as he remembered the conversation he needed to have with the chief.

"Could I have a word with you?" he asked.

Curiosity flickered in her gaze. "Of course."

As the two of them paced away from the crowd, Jimmy James filled her in about what had happened last night.

A knot formed between her eyes. "Is there anything you have for me that might identify them?"

"I got the HIN on the boat. I don't know if they had anything to do with what happened to Captain Bridgemore, but I wanted to let you know."

"Good job, Jimmy James. Text me that serial number you got from the boat, in case they decide to come back this way and cause more trouble." She scanned the crew in the distance. "Are you sure you're up for this adventure?"

As he glanced back over and spotted Kenzie retrieving her suitcase, he nodded. She was pretty much the reason that he was doing this. "It will be a nice change of pace."

The skin around her eyes crinkled as she studied him. "I never took you as a captain."

"I've been saving my money and setting some new goals. You know I've been trying to turn my life around for a long time now."

"You've been doing a great job. I'm really proud of you."

Her words caused warmth to spread through his chest. "Thanks, Chief."

She took a step back. "Anytime. I'd say call me if you have any trouble while you're out there, but you're going to be out of my jurisdiction."

"If there's one thing I've learned through my life it's how to handle myself in tough situations."

Her gaze locked with his. "Promise me you won't get yourself in trouble in the process."

He nodded. "I promise."

CHAPTER SEVEN

AS JIMMY JAMES—CAPTAIN Gamble as Kenzie should now call him—addressed the deckhands while they stood on the dock in front of *Almost Paradise*, Sunni leaned closer to Kenzie.

"This isn't going to be an easy trip, you know," she whispered.

"I'm not afraid of working hard." Kenzie raised her chin, wondering what all this hostility stemmed from.

She'd been around enough mean girls in her life to spot one. Unfortunately, Sunni definitely fell into that category. Insecurity masked with overconfidence. Center of attention tendencies. A know-it-all attitude.

She was going to be a peach to work with.

"You'll be up at the crack of dawn and not get to bed until after the sun sets," Sunni continued. "Are you prepared for that?"

Kenzie raised her chin. "I'll do whatever I need to do to get the job done."

Her cold stare still met Kenzie's. "I hope so. Because there's nothing I hate more than a lazy crew member. I like to envision myself throwing them overboard."

Kenzie flinched. Sunni nearly sounded threatening. *Throwing them overboard?*

She swallowed hard, trying to push down the uneasiness bubbling inside her.

Kenzie didn't want to form bad feelings toward this woman right from the start. If things stayed on schedule, the two of them would be together for the next eight weeks. But this conversation wasn't a good way to begin their working relationship.

Thankfully, Jimmy James joined them at that moment. Instead of seeming like the burly dock-worker she'd met yesterday, right now he seemed totally in charge of the situation as he looked at the papers in his hands and began to dole out assignments to get this boat in working order.

As everyone scattered to attend to their tasks,

Jimmy James called to Kenzie. She paused on the dock.

He stared down at her, his brown eyes full of concern. "How are you doing this morning?"

The concern in his voice made her cheeks heat. "I'm still a little shaken from last night, but I'm fine. I feel like I need to tell you thank you again—"

He raised a hand to stop her. "There's no need for that. I'm just glad that I was there when I was."

She glanced in the direction the thugs had disappeared last night and wondered what those guys were doing now.

"They're gone," he answered as if reading her mind.

"I suppose that's good." Her voice caught. "I just hope we don't run into them again."

"Same here." Jimmy James reached into his pocket and pulled something out. "By the way, I found something this morning."

Kenzie's eyes widened when she saw her mom's earring there. She quickly grabbed it and studied the diamond for any signs it had been damaged. But she didn't see anything.

"I can't believe you found it." She sounded nearly breathless as she said the words.

Jimmy James nodded. "I happened to be here early this morning, so I thought I'd take a look."

"Thank you so much." She started to reach for him, instinctively wanting to give him a hug. But she stopped herself.

This man was now her captain, and she needed to keep professional boundaries in place.

"It's no problem," Jimmy James said. "I'm glad I could help."

Kenzie stared up at him another moment, feeling like she should say more. Feeling like she wanted to sit down with this man and ask him questions and find out all about his life.

But before any inquiries left her lips, Jimmy James stepped back. "We've got to get this boat ready. The guests will be here before we know it."

Kenzie nodded, quickly putting her thoughts back into the proper place. Jimmy James wasn't her friend. He was her superior.

Besides, this job very well might take everything out of her. But she was going to prove she could handle being a steward on this yacht if it was the last thing that she did.

THE CREW SPENT the next two hours scrubbing the boat, preparing guest cabins, and ensuring they were stocked with enough food and drinks for the trip. While they did that, Jimmy James took the time to familiarize himself with the controls on the bridge.

This entire charter was a big undertaking, but Jimmy James felt prepared. This was what he wanted to do. He'd spent the last several years working on the docks and serving on various charters. Both had been fun. But it wasn't something he wanted to do for the rest of his life.

Before his dad died, Jimmy James had promised his father he'd make something of his life. He was going to see that promise through.

Just as he'd told Cassidy, he'd been saving his money the past few years. He'd used part of that to complete his USCG captain's training to receive his license. He'd also tucked some away for his future dreams.

While the rest of the crew continued to shine and polish everything, he reviewed the itinerary left for him by Mr. Robertson. *Almost Paradise* would depart today and go north to dock in Virginia Beach. Their guests wanted to spend a day exploring the area.

From there, they'd head up to Cape Charles so the group could play in the Chesapeake Bay.

Next, they'd hit Baltimore and the nightlife there. By the time they completed all that, it would be time to head back to Lantern Beach.

Most people who took these charter trips wanted to go to somewhere tropical, like the Mediterranean or the Caribbean. But some wanted to stay closer to home. Trips through New England were popular as well as some that left from Florida.

Although Lantern Beach seemed like an unlikely choice for a home port, when Jimmy James saw the price tag on this trip, he'd noticed it was cheaper than other charters. He wondered if Mr. Robertson had offered some type of price break since he was just starting this charter business and wanted to get some experience under his wing.

Jimmy James didn't know, and he supposed that wasn't his business. Mostly, he was in charge of safely transporting guests and crew as well as ensuring that everyone had a good time.

With the wind speeds at only seven to nine knots and no storms in the forecast, he anticipated the first leg of the trip would be smooth. But he'd closely monitor the weather for the duration of the charter.

When people paid high dollar for a trip like this, they expected the best. Not only that, but such patrons were generally wealthy and accustomed to being pampered.

A moment of doubt niggled in the back of his head when he realized the vast difference between the guests on this boat and himself.

Jimmy James hadn't grown up with much. His dad had been a fisherman, and most evenings they'd eaten whatever his dad caught that day. They didn't have a nice house, and half of the time their car hadn't run. But that didn't mean Jimmy James had a bad childhood, either. Hard at times, yes. But not bad.

Jimmy James paced to the window of the bridge and studied the deckhands as they worked, getting a feel for their experience levels and work ethic.

His gaze stopped on Eddie.

Something about him bothered Jimmy James, but he couldn't pinpoint what. Was it the cockiness in his gaze?

Maybe. He'd try to reserve his opinion for later.

Right now, Jimmy James had to keep his crew on the ball. Because even though Jimmy James said yes to this assignment because of Kenzie, he knew if he wanted any type of career within the charter boat industry that he had to give his best.

That's exactly what he intended on doing.

CHAPTER EIGHT

WHILE KENZIE WIPED down all the surfaces in the main salon—the primary indoor space for the guests—her gaze continued to travel back to the center of the teakwood floor. The area where she had found Captain Bridgemore.

Every time she closed her eyes, she pictured the blood there. Saw his lifeless body. Felt a jolt of fear.

She was thankful she hadn't been the one to clean up the blood. Jimmy James had taken care of that task before he'd gone to the bridge. Now, as she looked around the area, one wouldn't be able to tell what had happened if they didn't already know.

She prayed she'd made the right choice when she'd accepted this job. But as the time came closer for *Almost Paradise* to go out to sea, she questioned herself.

Instead of dwelling on her doubts, she tried to focus on the tasks at hand. As a steward, she would need to keep the interior of this yacht clean.

Almost Paradise had four decks. The lower deck was where the crew quarters were located—bunkrooms they shared with another coworker—as well as the crew mess. The engine room was also tucked away there.

The main deck contained the guest staterooms, a small salon, the galley, and a dining room. An outdoor hot tub and lounge area rounded out the space.

The upper deck held the main salon, a game room, and a meeting room/office area in case guests wanted to work while aboard. The bridge was toward the front of the boat as well, along with the captain's quarters.

Finally, the sun deck stretched atop the boat and primarily featured a lounge area.

Kenzie mentally reviewed the list of people who'd be guests this week. Each crew member had been given a preference sheet with photos of each guest, along with bios, meal preferences, allergies, and a wish-list of items they would like to do onboard.

A twenty-one-year-old named Buster Moreno was the primary guest. He had bleached-blond hair he wore tousled. His nose was on the larger side, and the remnants of acne scarred his jawline. But his sparkling eyes outshone any of his other traits. He'd become a YouTube sensation over the past four years because of his outrageous stunts.

His most popular videos were of him wing-walking on an airplane, supergluing his eyelids together, and letting mousetraps snap all over his skin.

Would he try to pull something here on the boat?

Kenzie had no doubt that Jimmy James could handle him if he did. Still, it could end up being a headache for the rest of them.

Joining Buster was Sylvia, his mom. She'd been a Walmart cashier up until two years ago when her son had bought her a nice house, and now he pretty much paid most of her expenses.

According to an internet article, she'd recently married a used car salesman named Gilbert, who would also be joining them. Looking at his picture, he still gave off that sleazy vibe, even if that was a stereotype—something that Kenzie generally hated.

Nikki Blanchard, Buster's latest girlfriend, would also be aboard. She was blonde with a small waist and a busty profile, almost reminding Kenzie of a young Pamela Anderson. She worked in real estate. Apparently, Buster liked to go through women like some people went through his YouTube videos.

His best friend, Waldo Alves, would also be there, acting as sidekick and part-time cameraman. Waldo was on the shorter side with longish black hair, and he appeared to have some type of Asian heritage.

Rounding out the group was Laney, Buster's eleven-year-old sister.

This was going to be an interesting week. Kenzie had always found people fascinating. But she didn't like drama, especially not when she was caught in the middle of it.

That was partly why it had been so hard when her dad married Leesa. Leesa was all about drama. The woman—who was only ten years older than Kenzie—owned a clothing boutique. The place didn't make any money, but Kenzie's dad helped to foot the bills, all because it "gave Leesa's life meaning."

Leesa was the opposite of Kenzie's mom, a down-to-earth nurse who'd insisted on living modestly. On the other hand, the first thing Leesa had done after getting married was to buy an extravagant house that "matched their place of prominence in the community."

Kenzie's heart sagged at the thought of it.

Before she could dwell on those thoughts anymore, Jimmy James emerged from the bridge and announced the guests' quickly approaching arrival. He instructed the crew to change into their uniforms and line up on the dock to greet them.

Kenzie quickly stowed her cleaning supplies in the closet and changed into a white skirt and a white polo top, the uniform given to her by Sunni. She had five different ones she'd wear on this trip, depending on the occasion.

As she headed back upstairs to greet the guests, all she could think was, here goes nothing.

THESE GUESTS WERE GOING to be a handful, Jimmy James mused. Tonight had proven that.

Buster was obnoxious and liked to be center of attention. Even worse, he constantly had his camera out and videoed himself doing even the smallest task. The people around him were all enablers. Clearly, Buster paid most of the bills for them and therefore was in control.

The only person who might be an exception to that enabling was Laney. But she was so busy playing a handheld video game that she didn't really care what else happened.

For the most part, the crew had done okay. They definitely had room to improve. But that was to be expected on the season's first charter.

The boat headed north and would dock in Virginia Beach for the night. Their guests wanted to enjoy the yacht's amenities on their first evening onboard.

For dinner, Chef Durango had prepared some fresh-caught tuna with risotto and roasted broccoli. Sunni and Kenzie had done a good job at both serving and cleaning up.

It was past eleven by the time they'd reached the port and docked for the evening.

Once Jimmy James saw that everything was under control, he stepped toward the captain's quarters directly behind the bridge. He wasn't ready to go to bed yet—not until he felt confident all the jobs were done. But he did want to get a feel for his cabin and unpack.

Stepping into the room, he scanned the space. It was smaller than he would have liked. Still, he'd seen the crew's accommodations and he knew he couldn't complain.

He unzipped the bag he'd thrown on his bed earlier and then walked to the dresser to open the first drawer. He put his T-shirts there. As he opened the second drawer, he must have jerked on it too hard. The entire compartment flew out.

He muttered beneath his breath as he picked the drawer up, ready to slide it back on the track.

As he did that, something inside the dresser caught his eye. Something that had been shoved to the back. Maybe it had fallen out of a drawer.

He knelt to get a better look. But it was dark at the back of the dresser, especially considering the dim light of the room.

He reached in and pulled out an envelope. When he opened it, he saw a wad of cash inside.

His eyes widened.

There had to be at least five thousand dollars here.

He rifled through the bills one more time, his heart pounding harder.

At the very end of the stash was a folded piece of paper. Written on the outside was "Captain," and inside it said, "Silence is golden."

His breath caught.

Was Captain Bridgemore being paid off to stay quiet about something? Was that the real reason he'd died? Maybe the fact that his wallet and phone had been stolen was simply a smokescreen for what was really going on.

Until Jimmy James knew more, it was hard to say.

Right now, he needed to call Cassidy. He also needed to keep his eyes wide open for trouble.

This boat shouldn't be called *Almost Paradise*.

Far from Paradise seemed like a better name.

CHAPTER NINE

KENZIE FELT the exhaustion pulling at her. She'd known this job would be hard work, and it definitely was. She'd been on her feet all day.

It was now past midnight, and she'd finally finished straightening up the salon.

More than anything, Kenzie just wanted to climb into bed and fall asleep. But she dreaded being in the small room with Sunni.

The bunkroom was probably only eight feet long and four feet wide. Just big enough to fit a set of bunkbeds and a couple of dressers. But there was no space for anything else. The attached bathroom was tiny too. Just big enough to turn around in, it seemed.

Kenzie would grab her things and hop in the shower before crawling into bed.

If her gut feeling was right, tomorrow was going to end up being a lot like today. Still, the hard work would be good for her, and she wasn't afraid of it.

As she pushed her door open, she braced herself for what could be a confrontation with her hostile roommate.

When she peered inside, Sunni wasn't there. Sunni and the rest of the crew were probably hanging out somewhere—without her. Kenzie knew that the world of charter cruising was small. Clearly, everyone else had already formed friendships.

She stepped farther into the room, ready to grab her bag when she paused.

Apprehension pricked her skin until goose-bumps rose.

What had caused this feeling?

When she glanced around, she saw that her suit-case was unzipped.

But she hadn't opened it since she had arrived. She was certain of it.

That meant someone else had been snooping through her things.

Carefully, she nudged the suitcase all the way open and stared at the contents inside.

The clothes she'd neatly folded were definitely disheveled.

Somebody *had* gone through her things. But why? What sense did that make?

The good thing—she wasn't sure *good* was the word she wanted to use—about being on this boat was that there were a limited number of possible suspects. Just the people onboard now.

Had another crew member done this? Or maybe one of Buster's people? Had he gone through her things for a YouTube video or something?

She startled as another thought hit her. Quickly, she opened her dresser drawer. Alarm raced through her.

She'd left her earrings there, afraid she might lose them. One of the backs was clearly loose.

But now they were gone.

Had the person who'd gone through her suitcase taken them?

Kenzie nibbled on her bottom lip. She thought about confronting Sunni, but she decided to wait instead. She'd keep her eyes open for any more signs of trouble.

She didn't know what was going on. But suddenly, this adventure she'd pursued in order to prove herself seemed like it was becoming a worse and worse idea.

JIMMY JAMES TOOK one last stroll around the boat to make sure everything was in place before he turned in for the night. Owen would take night shift, watching to make sure everyone behaved, was safe, and that no one uninvited tried to board the vessel.

As he went to the upper deck, he saw that Buster and his friends were laughing and drinking entirely too much. It wasn't surprising. People tended to do that when they chartered this kind of boat. But Jimmy James knew firsthand the stupid kinds of things alcohol could lead to.

He spoke to them a few minutes before telling them good night. The main deck appeared empty, but he started toward the stern just to be sure.

He paused by the door when he spotted Eddie and Sunni on the bow. The two of them leaned on the railing and spoke in low tones to each other.

He knew he shouldn't eavesdrop, but he couldn't seem to stop himself.

"What do you think of the new girl?" Sunni whispered.

"I guess she seems nice enough. A little green, though."

"I'll whip her into shape. By the end of this she'll either be the world's best stew or she'll be running for the hills. I'll make sure of that."

The two exchanged a grin as if they enjoyed torturing their fellow crewmates.

Jimmy James stepped out of the shadows. "Everything going okay out here?"

Sunni and Eddie both straightened as if wanting to appear like they hadn't been gossiping.

"Everything is fine." Eddie rolled a shoulder back. "Just enjoying a little late-night conversation."

"Good to hear," Jimmy James said. "Anything I need to know about?"

The two of them exchanged another glance before Eddie said, "I thought today went pretty well, all things considered."

Jimmy James nodded. "It did. Good work. Now let's keep this going for the rest of the trip."

Something flashed in Eddie's eyes.

Defiance. Not necessarily defiance about what Jimmy James had just talked to him about, but just a general rebellion.

That trait seemed to define Eddie, and that was

going to be a problem. Jimmy James would confront him about it if it came down to it.

But it was more than that. Jimmy James sensed that those two were hiding something. That they had secrets.

Did those secrets have anything to do with Captain Bridgemore's death?

Not necessarily.

But until Jimmy James figured out what these two might be up to, he was going to remain on guard.

CHAPTER TEN

BUSTER HAD REQUESTED a full beach extravaganza the next day—a schedule that Kenzie couldn't help but think was sure to exhaust the crew.

Eddie and his team had set the anchor offshore in Virginia Beach and transported the guests to land on the small tender boat. They found a quiet, private beach for a picnic complete with plenty of alcohol.

Buster had wanted homemade sushi to eat on the beach, where he could gloat to any nearby fish that he was eating their family—his words. Afterward, he wanted to take an excursion to the resort area to ride a four-seater Surrey cycle bike and then parasail.

In the evening, he wanted to hit the club scene and had requested that Sunni watch Laney for them.

Kenzie knew Sunni wasn't thrilled about the idea, yet she'd been unable to say no. On cruises like this, guests usually got their way.

The good news was that Kenzie's earrings had magically reappeared in her dresser this morning after she'd gotten back from serving breakfast.

She still wasn't sure how it had happened. Part of her felt like she was losing her mind. Or maybe someone was playing mind games.

Kenzie didn't know. But she was so grateful to have her earrings back. She put them in a compartment in her suitcase and prayed they'd stay safe there.

She couldn't bear the thought of losing them.

She hadn't confronted Sunni about potentially being the one who'd messed with her things, but Kenzie's encounters with Sunni remained terse. The woman showed no warmth to her nor did she cut her any slack—not that Kenzie thought she *should* cut her slack. Still, Kenzie wasn't sure how the two of them had gotten started on the wrong foot as they seemed to.

While everyone else played in the water, Nikki paced closer to Kenzie and Siv who were cleaning up from lunch. Kenzie braced herself for another request—some ice-cold water with only three ice cubes or a piece of sushi that was perfectly round and not misshapen.

"What do you think about what happened to our first captain?" Worry strained her voice.

"We wouldn't have come on this cruise if we thought you were in danger," Siv said. "I know it's worrisome, but I feel confident that the police are handling it."

Nikki nodded. "It's hard not to think about it. Why would someone kill him?"

Siv shrugged. "What do they say? Most murders happen for either love or money. In this case, it appears someone really wanted his wallet."

"Why target him?"

Siv seemed comfortable taking over these questions, so Kenzie let him. He nodded toward *Almost Paradise* in the distance.

"The yacht itself makes an easy target," he said. "People see it and assume anyone associated with it is wealthy. I'm sure that was the reason why."

That seemed to appease Nikki for a moment.

She opened her mouth as if she wanted to ask another question. Before she could, Buster called to her from the water, motioning for her to come join him.

Nikki shrugged before splashing through the water toward him.

The woman had every right to be worried. In fact, if she wasn't worried then that would be weird. Not only that, but her concerns were valid. Kenzie felt those same worries deep inside her.

———————

JIMMY JAMES PAUSED in his room and glanced around.

He strode to his bed and frowned.

The book he'd been reading was gone.

He was certain he'd left it on his nightstand.

Most people didn't think of him as a reader—and he hadn't always been—but he found the act helped to center him. He'd been working his way through the Lord of the Rings trilogy, trying to read a chapter each night.

So where had his book gone?

He looked on the floor, checking to see if the book had somehow fallen.

But it was nowhere to be seen.

His frown deepened.

Had someone been in his room? And, if so, why would they steal his book? It made no sense.

He looked through the rest of his belongings, and everything was still there—even the five thousand dollars he'd found in the dresser.

His back muscles bristled.

This was one more thing he'd need to keep his eyes on.

But he didn't like the overall picture that was beginning to form.

CHAPTER ELEVEN

AFTER THE BEACH EXCURSION, the crew scrambled to bring everything back to *Almost Paradise* and get it put away while preparing for the next stage of Buster's adventures.

Working as a yachtie—a term some considered demeaning, but it didn't bother Kenzie—was definitely exhausting, and she'd only just started.

As she grabbed an armful of towels and started toward the laundry, she paused near the galley as an unrecognizable voice drifted out.

Who was that?

She didn't want to eavesdrop, yet she couldn't seem to help herself.

"I know, right?" the unknown voice said. "This is the opportunity of a lifetime."

Opportunity of a lifetime?

"I'm definitely going to make the most of it," the person continued, clearly on the phone since Kenzie couldn't hear any responses. "Nothing—and no one—is going to get in my way."

Was that because this person had killed whoever might stop him? Could that person have been Captain Bridgemore?

She peered in the galley, remaining quiet and desperate to remain unseen. But she had to see who was talking.

She sucked in a breath when she saw who was inside.

Durango.

His French accent had been gone when she'd overheard him talking.

As he started to turn, she quickly ducked out of sight. She didn't think he'd seen her.

But what had that conversation been about?

And why was he faking an accent?

JIMMY JAMES STOOD in the background, observing everything taking place around him as the crew and guests got ready for their excursion into the resort area of Virginia Beach.

The coastal city contained some private beaches, but they also had a bustling resort area filled with tall hotels, a small amusement park, clubs, and plenty of other entertainment.

Jimmy James himself preferred the quiet of Lantern Beach. He preferred a sandy shore where he could set up camp for the day without sitting crowded with hundreds of other people.

But everyone had different tastes. Virginia Beach did have some great restaurants, an awesome board-walk, and lots of concerts in the summertime.

As Buster turned to Waldo and said something to him, Jimmy James watched them. Buster's camera was out—of course—recording everything that happened.

"What do you think about parasailing?" Buster asked, camera pointed at the two of them.

Waldo shrugged. "Is that when two people go sailing?"

Buster cackled. "No, it's when you're pulled behind a boat and go up in the air with a parachute type of canopy. Are you up for that?"

"Do I have a choice?" Waldo looked honestly confused.

"You either go up in the air or your career will be up in the air." Buster cackled again. "You got that, buddy?"

While Waldo seemed to pause and formulate an answer, Buster rolled his eyes on camera, letting anyone who was watching know that he didn't think his friend was very smart.

But, in real life, Waldo didn't seem as clueless as he did on the screen. Jimmy James supposed that was part of their schtick. Still, it almost seemed like any self-respecting person wouldn't stand for something like this.

He supposed it wasn't his concern.

But he planned to keep an eye on everyone on this boat . . . just to be safe.

CHAPTER TWELVE

IT WASN'T until Buster and his crew went out for a night of clubbing that Kenzie felt like she could breathe. They'd been cleaning, doing laundry, preparing food, and serving guests all day. But now she actually had a couple of hours of quiet before the guests returned and needed to be waited on.

Sunni was with Laney, and Eddie was in charge of picking up Buster and his posse when they were ready.

Kenzie wasn't sure where the rest of the crew was. It didn't really matter to her right now. Instead, she sat on the swim platform at the stern of the boat, looking out over the water and Virginia Beach in the background. The lights from the tall hotels made a striking skyline, and the rhythm of the waves instantly put her soul at ease.

"Do you mind if I join you?" a deep voice said behind her.

She looked up and saw Jimmy James. Her breath caught at the sight of him. There was just something about his presence . . . his imposing frame. His muscles. His confidence.

For better or worse, the man fascinated her.

"Of course not, Captain." She patted the space beside her.

A smile flickered across his face when she used his title. He almost looked like he wanted to rebuke the words before realizing he shouldn't. Professionally, that's what Kenzie needed to call him while they were working.

He lowered himself beside her, his legs dangling over the water. A moment of peace fell over them. If she could bottle this moment, she might.

"Can I ask you a question?" Kenzie turned toward Jimmy James.

"Go ahead—just be gentle with me."

She smiled at his self-deprecating tone. "Is there any reason why you go by Jimmy James?"

"My dad told my mom that there's no reason to have a middle name unless you planned to use it. So, ever since I can remember, that's what my parents called me. It stuck. Now, if someone calls me Jimmy, it doesn't even register that they're talking to me."

"That makes sense."

"My turn to ask a question now?"

She swallowed hard, not wanting to seem like she was hiding anything but not comfortable opening up either. Despite that, she said, "Sure."

"Why are you here, Kenzie?" His voice dipped low, any humor disappearing from his tone.

She glanced at Jimmy James, surprised by his question.

She took a sip of water as she contemplated what —and how much—to say. Finally, she offered, "Truth be told, I'm supposed to go back to med school in the fall."

"Med school?" His eyebrows shot in the air. "What happened?"

She shrugged. "I guess I realized I was following this plan other people had laid out for me. But I don't want to follow in my father's footsteps. I don't want to be a doctor or a surgeon one day."

"Your dad is a doctor?"

She nodded. "That's right. A brain surgeon. He's acclaimed—he flies out all over the world to perform surgeries."

"Impressive. I take it you don't enjoy the medical field?"

She shrugged. "I see how much of his schedule is consumed by his work. He does important things, don't get me wrong. But he was absent most of my childhood. I don't want that for my future."

"Could you just become a general practitioner instead? Something less demanding?"

She leaned back onto the palms of her hands as she considered his question. "Maybe. But it's just really not what I want."

"What *do* you want, Kenzie?"

She glanced at the dark sky above and the lapping waves around her. "*This* is what I want. One of the only times I feel at peace is when I'm out here on the water."

"So, you want to work on charter boats the rest of your life? Or you want to buy your own boat and set out on the ultimate adventure?"

She shrugged. "I'm not sure. But I know I don't want to be a doctor. We've only got one chance at this life, you know? I have to follow my own path, even if that path disappoints my dad."

"That's true."

She bent her head toward the water as her thoughts turned somber. "My mom died eight years ago. She was fine one moment, and a heart attack took her life the next. My dad wasn't there. He was in Indiana doing a surgery, so he couldn't save her."

"I'm sorry, Kenzie." His voice sounded soft with compassion.

"I didn't realize it until I was older, but losing my mom made me realize how short life is. I don't have time to follow other people's dreams. What about what makes me happy?"

"You should be happy." Jimmy James' voice held what almost sounded like a declaration. "You can't let other people dictate your life."

She looked up at him, gratitude swelling inside her. "Thank you for understanding."

"Thank you for sharing."

This guy was so different than most of the people she'd ever hung out with. So why did it feel so easy to talk to him? Why did she feel such a quick bond?

She wasn't sure. But she was thankful he'd wandered into her life when he did.

AS JIMMY JAMES listened to Kenzie's story, more pieces of her life fell into place in his mind. It made more sense why she was here. But he had a feeling she still had secrets, that there was more to the story.

He supposed he could say that about anybody though. Most people didn't spill their entire life to people they'd only met the day before.

"What about you?" Kenzie looked up at him with wide brown eyes that beckoned him to open up. "What's your story?"

At her question, a weight formed on his chest. Jimmy James would like to say that he could share his past without fear of judgment. But that wasn't true.

Especially when it came to good girls like Kenzie Anderson. Women like her wouldn't understand.

He couldn't even blame them for that.

"I hit a rough patch several years ago, but I've been trying to get back on the straight and narrow ever since. Every day I like to say I make a little bit of progress." His answer was vague, but would it be enough to satisfy her curiosity?

"How do you define rough patch?"

That was exactly what he was afraid Kenzie might ask.

He let out a breath, knowing that there was no shame in owning up to your shortcomings and mistakes. "I got involved with some drugs. I'm not proud of it. At the time, I was working as a fisherman with my father and . . . let's just say the pay isn't great."

"I can imagine."

"I became desperate for more drugs, to get another hit, and that led me to do desperate things. Petty crimes mostly. I stole some things so I could buy more drugs, and I was eventually caught. I spent six months in jail. When I got out, I'd like to say that was my wake-up call. But it wasn't. Old habits are hard to break."

"What made you change?"

His chest tightened at the memories. "A friend of mine got hurt. I almost couldn't help her because I was so high. She could have died, and it would have been my fault if she had. I gave up drugs that day and never looked back."

A rush of emotions hit him at the thought, and his eyes warmed as moisture flooded them. He quickly rubbed the corners, trying to stop any tears from falling. But it happened every time he told that story. Even after all these years, regret still filled him.

Kenzie stared up at him. He expected to see judgment in her gaze. Instead, compassion filled her eyes as she offered a gentle smile. "Thank you for sharing. I realize that probably wasn't easy, but I appreciate it."

"Of course."

Kenzie shifted as she turned toward him, something changing in her gaze.

"Captain Gamble . . ." Kenzie's voice trailed as she pressed her lips together.

"Yes?" His breath caught as he waited to hear what she had to say.

She licked her lips as if contemplating her words. "When I got down to my room last night, I discovered that someone had gone through my suitcase."

His spine tightened. "What?"

"I wasn't sure if I should say anything—"

"You should *always* say something," he told her. "Why didn't you come to me earlier?"

"The crew . . . they already don't like me. Me being a snitch isn't going to help the situation."

He knew what it was like to be an outsider, but he doubted someone like Kenzie was familiar with the feeling. "It's not being a snitch if you're being honest. Was anything taken?"

"I thought my earrings were missing, but then I found them again." She let out a sigh. "I'm not sure why anyone would go through my things unless maybe they're trying to learn more about me. Trying to find some . . . I don't know. Trying to find some secrets or something." She shrugged.

Jimmy James stared at her another moment, a surge of worry rushing through him. He didn't like the sound of this.

"If anything else happens, you tell me." He looked her in the eyes. "Okay? No fears about being a tattletale."

She nibbled on her bottom lip as she nodded, her uncertainty still present. "I will. I promise."

"And I wouldn't worry so much about the crew not liking you. They just don't know you yet. Give them time."

"I'm not really worried about it." Kenzie shrugged. "It's more of an observation. But thank you."

He stared at her another moment, some type of internal instinct beckoning him to reach out and place his hand on her back.

But before he could, his radio crackled and a voice came over the airwaves. It was a message from Eddie. Buster was ready to come back to the boat.

Maybe it was better this way. Because it had stopped Jimmy James from doing something that he might regret.

CHAPTER THIRTEEN

IF THE CREW had been expecting a relaxing, peaceful night, they were wrong.

Buster decided that he and his friends wanted to do some karaoke. They'd already been drinking entirely too much. At least Laney was safely tucked in bed and didn't have to see everything.

Unfortunately, Buster had requested that the crew join them.

Karaoke was the *last thing* Kenzie wanted to do, but she knew she couldn't get out of it. At least Jimmy James and the deckhands could because they were busy docking the boat for the evening.

Mostly, Kenzie tried to make herself invisible except for the occasional request for more food or drinks. Sunni, on the other hand, seemed to fit right in. She had no problem getting up and singing songs, including a couple of duets with Buster.

As everyone had laughed and sang, Kenzie glanced around the room. Buster's mother sat off to the side, looking a little calmer than the rest of the group. The woman kept touching the diamond necklace gracing her neck.

Kenzie wondered if her son had bought her the jewelry once he'd made it big-time. The diamond was huge and didn't seem like something she'd want to wear out in public. She supposed it could have sentimental value, kind of like Kenzie's earrings.

Was this Buster guy really making that much money?

Kenzie knew the answer was yes. She'd looked him up earlier today. According to online reports, he brought in about ten million dollars every year from doing his videos. It seemed like an insane amount of money to make simply from doing stupid things, but she supposed that was the nature of a free market.

Her gaze moved from Buster's mom to Buster's best friend, Waldo. He was quiet, the serious guy to Buster's egregious personality. From what Kenzie had seen, this guy seemed to do whatever Buster told him to do. He was definitely a wingman and not the star of the show.

Kenzie had to wonder if he ever resented Buster for always putting him on the backburner. Maybe not, but she did have to wonder how those dynamics would work.

Her face heated when Buster paused in front of her holding a microphone. He reached out to take her hand. "It's your turn."

As panic rushed through her, Kenzie shook her head. "Oh, no. I don't sing."

"But I want you to." He waggled his eyebrows. "Besides, you're working for me. You have to do what I say."

Alarms sounded in her head. Kenzie didn't like it when people tried to force her to do anything. "I'm fine, really."

"You need to sing," Sunni hissed in her ear. "It's not a big deal. Just do it."

She glanced at the woman, who was technically her boss. Dread welled in her, but she finally nodded. Fighting this would only make it worse.

"Why not?" Kenzie tried to lighten her voice, despite the trepidation coursing through her.

Buster grinned. "I have just the song for you to sing. You ever watch *The Little Mermaid*?"

"I have."

"Let's give it up for Steward Kenzie singing

'Under the Sea.' Make it good because I'm recording this!"

Great. She was going to end up on his YouTube channel, wasn't she?

Everyone cheered as she went to the front of the room with a microphone in hand.

As she did, her gaze wandered to the other side of the salon where Buster's stepdad, Gilbert, stared at his phone, his expression tense. Instead of joining in the festivities, he slipped from the room.

What was that about? Kenzie wondered.

She rubbed her throat, apprehension filling her at the thought of having to sing in public—and disappointment over the fact that she wouldn't be able to figure out where Gilbert had gone. Not now, at least.

———

JIMMY JAMES WALKED past the main salon in time to hear Kenzie crooning a song from some cartoon, if he remembered correctly.

He cringed as he listened. She wasn't very good. Then again, doing karaoke probably hadn't been her idea.

As he glanced through the glass divider separating the room from the hallway, he noted how uncomfortable Kenzie looked as she stood on a makeshift stage. With one hand, she held a microphone. With the other, she held the tips of her hair. Her gaze was focused on a monitor in front of her as if she didn't want to miss a word of the song.

Meanwhile, Sunni stood in the corner with a smirk on her face. It was clear to Jimmy James exactly what happened here.

Sunni had put Kenzie up to this. His gut clinched at the thought.

Kenzie finished singing and offered a gracious bow. At least she didn't take herself too seriously.

With one last glance, he continued onto the deck and glanced at another boat three slips down.

A scrawny man stood talking to someone in low tones. It was hard to make out many details, but Jimmy James thought he could see dark hair and angular features. The guy was maybe in his twenties.

Something about him seemed familiar. But unless he got closer for a better look, he wouldn't know what that was.

He glanced at the wooden slip leading to *Almost Paradise*, tempted to go right now and see why he'd recognize somebody all the way up here in Virginia Beach.

But before he could do that, his radio crackled. "Sunni, Sunni. Cleanup on aisle four."

It was Eddie trying to be funny.

Saying a person's name twice to get their attention was common for VHF, also known as maritime radio.

"Someone barfed on the top deck," Eddie continued. "Need a mop ASAP."

Jimmy James stepped away from the railing, his thoughts still heavy.

The person who'd killed the captain was still out there. Had the murderer gotten what he or she wanted? Was it all to steal the captain's wallet or the cash found in the dresser? If so, why come all the way to Lantern Beach to do that?

Unless it was someone who was already hanging around and had seen the opportunity.

At that thought, Jimmy James realized the circle of suspects was getting smaller and smaller.

If it was someone hanging out at the docks, it might be someone he'd seen before . . . or maybe even someone he knew.

He didn't like the thought of that.

CHAPTER FOURTEEN

AS KENZIE SET the table for breakfast, an agitated voice sounded down the hallway.

"Where is he? Has anyone seen him?"

She glanced up as Buster stormed onto the aft deck. His eyes blazed and his motions looked frantic as he scanned the area.

She set the stack of linen napkins down and stepped toward him, worried something was seriously wrong. "Is everything okay?"

He sighed, not bothering to hide his agitation as he turned toward her. "Have you seen Waldo?"

"Not since last night at karaoke."

He raked a hand through his hair. "I went to get him this morning so we could edit my video, but he wasn't in his room. I've searched the boat, and I can't find him."

Setting the table suddenly didn't seem as important. "I'll help. Maybe your paths just somehow missed each other."

Just then, Jimmy James stepped from the starboard side of the boat, seeming to have a sixth sense for trouble. He approached them, hands on his hips and a knot between his eyes.

"What's going on?" he asked.

"I can't find Waldo." Buster threw his hands in the air, his motions making him look like a ball of stress and anxiety. "I don't know where he went."

Jimmy James glanced at Kenzie as if trying to get her read on this situation. She shrugged, still unsure if Buster was exaggerating or not.

"Maybe he just took a walk," Kenzie said. "I'll go look."

"I'll get the rest of the crew to help," Jimmy James said. "I'm sure Waldo is around here somewhere."

"It doesn't seem like him to do this." Buster ran a hand through his hair, the first touch of sincere concern lacing his voice. "He's not even answering his phone. I need to get this video posted."

That was the last thing Kenzie heard as she started up to the top deck.

Was this some type of YouTube stunt? She wouldn't put it past Buster to do something like that. But he did seem truly upset.

Twenty minutes later, everybody met on the afterdeck, each reporting the same results.

Waldo was nowhere to be found.

It almost sounded like a bad joke, but it wasn't.

Jimmy James stood in front of everyone as he addressed the guests and crew. His chest seemed even broader as it puffed up with concern and as he took charge of the situation. The sun had fully risen, but smears of pink and yellow remained in the sky, reminding them that it was still early—even if it felt like hours had passed.

"When was the last time anyone saw him?" Jimmy James asked.

A round of "at karaoke" sounded around the deck. It appeared their guests had finished their evening with singing and then gone straight to bed, where most people had probably passed out from their over-consumption of alcohol. In fact, half the people here right now looked like they had a hangover.

"Nobody saw him after he went to his stateroom." Jimmy James put his hands on his hips as he scanned everyone's gazes. "Is that correct?"

"I saw him." Laney looked up from her video game, shrugged, and then kept playing.

Everyone's attention turned to her.

Jimmy James moved toward the girl and knelt in front of her. "Where did you see him, Laney?"

She shrugged. "I saw him walk off the boat. It was probably around two o'clock."

"What were you doing up at two a.m.?" Her mom's voice rose in agitation.

Laney's eyes widened. "You think I could sleep with all that karaoke going on? I'm good, but I'm not that good. You guys were terrible."

Kenzie had to smile. There was nothing funny about the situation, but the girl's comeback had seemed appropriate.

"Was he with anyone?" Jimmy James asked.

"No, he was alone."

"Did you see which direction he walked?"

"He headed toward the parking lot. When he disappeared, I went back to bed. I figured it wasn't my business."

"What about luggage?" Jimmy James continued. "Did he have anything with him?"

Laney shrugged. "I didn't see anything."

Jimmy James turned to Owen. "You were on duty last night. Did you see anything?"

Owen shook his head. "No, sorry, Captain. I didn't. But I was keeping my eye on the hot tub because I overheard Buster saying he was going to see how long he could hold his breath underwater. I didn't want to take any chances that he would come back out of his stateroom and try it."

That didn't sound out of the realm of possibility, Kenzie mused.

Jimmy James turned back to address the crowd again. "Is it like Waldo to just up and leave?"

Buster and his gang glanced at each other before shrugging.

"I wouldn't put it past him to do it," Sylvia finally said.

Kenzie glanced around. Where was Gilbert? Everyone else was here, but she'd just realized he was missing.

"Gilbert's allergies are acting up," Sylvia explained as if reading Kenzie's thoughts.

Kenzie nodded. But what if that was just an excuse? The man had a shifty gaze that made him seem untrustworthy.

Eddie squirmed beside her and rubbed his neck as if uncomfortable.

Jimmy James focused on him, picking up on his subtle discomfort. "Eddie? Do you have something to add?"

"I don't want to say anything inappropriate, Captain." He shrugged and almost looked sheepish.

Buster turned toward Eddie, his eyes narrow and agitation still seeping from him. "If you know something about Waldo, say it."

"I overheard an argument yesterday between Buster and Waldo," Eddie said. "Waldo said he had enough and that he was tired of playing the stupid friend in their little YouTube duo. He was upset because Buster makes all the big bucks and gets the fans, and Waldo is just known as the stupid sidekick."

Kenzie swerved her gaze back toward Buster to watch his reaction. To her surprise, he didn't deny it.

"We did get into a fight. It happens occasionally. But we settled it before I went to bed, and everything was fine."

"If this is no big deal, why didn't you mention it earlier?" Kenzie asked.

Buster frowned. "Because I knew how it would sound. Believe me, that argument had nothing to do with Waldo disappearing. I promise."

Kenzie wasn't so sure about that. She glanced

back at Jimmy James, whose gaze also narrowed with suspicion.

He would have to decide how to proceed from here. They were supposed to leave the harbor in two hours and move on to their next location.

Should they leave Waldo behind? Or should they assume he'd show back up before they departed?

She didn't envy the choice Jimmy James had to make.

WHILE BUSTER and his crew had breakfast—what Chef Durango could salvage from the meal he'd had to abandon earlier as everyone searched for Waldo —Jimmy James sent Eddie and Owen to look for Waldo in the harbor area. If they didn't find him, Jimmy James would call the police. Filing a report was only smart, especially in case this ordeal turned out to be anything other than Waldo leaving of his own volition.

He stood on the bridge to collect his thoughts, praying that he'd have wisdom in handling this situation. He grabbed a bottle of water and took a long sip to cool off. The day was already turning steamy —and that wasn't because of the weather.

He could see why Waldo might be upset with Buster. His friend didn't treat him very well. In the short time Jimmy James had been around them, he'd already noticed the lack of respect.

Buster got laughs by putting his friend down. On camera, Waldo seemed okay with it, like he was willing to take one for the team if it meant bringing in more money. But had resentment secretly been building deep down inside Waldo?

Or there was still the possibility that this was somehow tied in with everything that was happening with this boat. Jimmy James didn't know yet and needed more information before he could form an opinion on it.

"You think something's wrong too, don't you?"

He looked up when he heard the words and saw Kenzie at the door. She stepped closer to him, a concerned look on her face.

Anyone else he would have sent away—but not Kenzie. In fact, seeing her already made him feel better.

He didn't bother to deny her question about something being wrong. "I do. I don't like whatever it is that's going on."

"Do you think this has anything to do with Bridgemore?"

Jimmy James thought about the money and note he'd found in the captain's quarters. Thought about the fact Kenzie's bags had been gone through. Thought about all the whispering he'd heard between various parties while on the boat.

"It's really too early to say," Jimmy James finally told her. "But I'm going to keep my eyes wide open. You should too."

She nodded, almost a little too quickly. "Oh, believe me. I am. This charter had me on edge before it even started."

Just then, his phone rang, and a familiar number popped up on his screen. It was Leo Reynolds, a charter boat fishing captain he'd worked with before. Jimmy James had left a message for him earlier.

He glanced at Kenzie and excused himself. "I've got to take this."

Her eyes widened with perceptive curiosity. "Of course."

He waited until she'd exited the bridge before answering.

CHAPTER FIFTEEN

"HEY, LEO," Jimmy James started. "Thanks for giving me a call back."

He'd briefly worked as a first mate on Leo's fishing boat—a Viking 48 convertible named *Predator*. They'd had some great times deep sea fishing together and still maintained a good relationship.

"No problem. What's going on?" Leo's voice, hoarse from smoking too much, stretched across the line.

"I have a question for you that might sound odd. But did you ever meet or talk to someone named Larry Bridgemore?"

"He was the captain on *Almost Paradise*, right?"

Leo said. "Speaking of which, did I hear that you took over?"

Jimmy James' eyebrows flickered up. He shouldn't be surprised. Word did travel fast at the docks and on the boating circuit. "I did. It's a long story."

"That's impressive, my man. Takes a big person to take on a boat like that."

"I'm doing my best." Jimmy James didn't bother to mention that sometimes he felt he'd gotten in over his head. He could handle operating the boat. Trying to deal with the people onboard was a whole different story.

"What do you need to know about the captain?" Leo asked.

Jimmy James stared out the window at the rolling whitecaps. "I'm just trying to find more information on him. I'm sure you've heard by now that he was murdered."

"It's been all the talk in the fishing community. Heard it was a robbery gone bad."

Jimmy James wasn't too sure about that, but he didn't share that opinion with his friend. He'd leave that up to Chief Chambers if she saw fit to share the news.

"I did meet him a couple of times. I know he

likes Bermuda a lot, but he wanted to take on some higher-end charters. I did hear through the grapevine that he got himself into quite a bit of debt."

His breath caught. "Any idea how he got himself into debt?"

"Gambling. When he wasn't working, he liked to head up to Atlantic City. At least, that's what the rumor mill says. I'm not sure if that helps you or not. You think his gambling is linked to what happened to him?"

That was an excellent question—and one Jimmy James wasn't prepared to answer yet. "I can't say for sure. I'm just trying to collect all the information I can in case this somehow ties in with the boat."

But Jimmy James' mind remained on that wad of cash he'd found and the note with it saying silence is golden.

There was definitely something going on here.

Maybe he needed to dig into the backgrounds of everyone onboard this boat if he really wanted to find answers.

But what concerned him the most was when he thought about Kenzie. She was in the thick of things here on the boat, reminding him of a doe standing in the middle of the street watching the headlights head right toward her.

Not that Kenzie wasn't intelligent. But the woman clearly hadn't been around enough cunning people to know how to handle them. She screamed sheltered, sweet, and innocent.

He frowned.

Jimmy James would make sure that nothing happened to her if it was the last thing he did.

AN HOUR LATER, there was still no sign of where Waldo had gone. Even Buster couldn't seem to bring himself to make any jokes about the irony of that statement.

Everyone had gathered in the main salon to pass the time, but what they were really doing was commiserating.

Buster stared at his phone as if a message might pop up explaining the whole situation. His lower lip extended out in a subtle pout, and he kept muttering indiscernible things under his breath.

His mom sat on one side of him and his girl-friend, Nikki, on the other, both trying to comfort him. Meanwhile, stepdad Gilbert tried to break the mood by making slightly inappropriate and totally awkward jokes. Kenzie still thought the man was hiding something. She just wasn't sure what.

Either way, Kenzie hated to see how distressed they were, but she still hoped there might be a positive resolution. She hoped Waldo had simply gotten fed up and left for a while.

In the meantime, she and Sunni served drinks and brought snacks. Laney was teaching Jimmy James how to play one of her video games across the room. He was surprisingly good at interacting with her.

Thirty minutes into their time together, Buster finally raised his head, his eyes hardening as if he'd made up his mind. "We should leave without him."

"What?" Nikki muttered beside him, her voice sounding breathless with surprise.

Buster nodded, resolve solidifying in his eyes. "Waldo wants to ruin me. To make me think I'm nothing without him. *That's* what this is all about."

"You really think that he just walked away?" Jimmy James raised an eyebrow.

"I do." Buster crossed his arms. "He must have planned this after the fight we had last night. I thought we worked it out, but I guess not. I'll never forgive him for leaving me in a lurch like this."

"Leaving you in a lurch?" Kenzie repeated, curious about what that meant.

Buster looked back at her, irritation in his gaze. "Yeah, a lurch. I tried to edit and post a video this morning for my fans, and it turned out to be a disaster because that's usually Waldo's job."

No one said anything, but something unspoken seemed to linger in the air.

Finally, Buster shrugged, but the motion was stiff and agitated. "I know you guys think he's just my friend, but I *do* pay him. It's not like he's doing all this for free or out of the kindness of his heart."

"We can't leave him here." Nikki still gaped, sounding mortified at the thought.

Buster shrugged, bad attitude rising from him like fog off the water. "We're in Virginia Beach. Waldo has enough money to take an Uber all the way back to Raleigh if that's what he wants to do. He'll be fine."

Kenzie turned to Jimmy James, the peacemaker side of her kicking into action. "You called the police, right? What did they say?"

Jimmy James straightened. "I got off the phone with them before I came in. They said it's too early to officially file a missing person's report. By all appearances, Waldo left by his own free will."

Buster stood. "That settles it. This is *my* charter cruise, and I want to leave. *Now*."

Kenzie's shoulders tightened. She couldn't see herself ever leaving one of her friends behind in a situation like this. Any respect she'd felt toward Buster diminished.

She would keep doing the tasks she'd agreed to when she signed up for this charter. She'd serve food and drinks. Keep everything tidy. Work on laundry. She wouldn't make Jimmy James look bad or give Sunni the satisfaction of thinking Kenzie was a failure.

But Kenzie wouldn't enjoy any of it.

CHAPTER SIXTEEN

JIMMY JAMES FELT his jaw stiffen as he stood behind the helm and cruised across the water away from Virginia Beach.

As per Buster's wishes.

He didn't like this. He didn't like anything that was going on. The decision to leave hadn't been easy, and he still prayed he'd made the right choice. If Laney hadn't seen Waldo walk off the boat, his first concern would have been that Waldo could have fallen off the boat, hit his head, and now was adrift in the ocean.

A knock sounded at the door behind him, and he called, "Come in."

Kenzie stepped inside. Something about her

actions seemed tentative. Maybe it was the way she kept wetting her lips. Maybe it was her tense arms and shoulders or her hesitant steps.

"Do you have a minute?" she asked softly.

His heart skipped a beat at the sight of her. "For you? Of course. Come in. Shut the door behind you. Is everything okay?"

She paced over beside him and stared out over the water with a frown on her face. "I feel so horrible about leaving Waldo behind."

Her words took away any of the joy Jimmy James had felt after seeing Kenzie. The burst of pleasure had been short-lived. "I do too. But there's no evidence of a crime."

"I know but given everything that's happened . . ." Her frown deepened.

"I understand. I don't like it any more than you do."

She glanced at him, her inquiring eyes boring into his. "What do you think is going on here, Captain Gamble?"

He shook his head, not wanting to throw out any theories until he had more information. "I don't know. But there's more here than meets the eye. I'm certain of that."

Kenzie rubbed her arms as if chilled and stared out the window at the ocean around them again. "I feel like I just walked into the middle of something. I don't know what, and I don't know who is involved but . . ."

"You're scared," he finished.

She nodded somberly as she glanced at him again, appreciation in her gaze. She seemed to crave someone who understood her, to crave connection.

He could understand that.

"Yes, I'm scared," she said.

"Nothing wrong with being a little scared. It will keep you sharp."

Kenzie let out a long breath. "I shouldn't have ever taken this job, should I? I should have just gone on with life as expected and stayed in med school. Maybe Sunni is right, and I'm not cut out for this kind of work."

"If med school doesn't make you happy, then you shouldn't go back to med school. Don't get me wrong —happiness isn't everything in life, despite what some people believe."

Kenzie twisted her neck as she scrutinized his expression, looking as if she hadn't expected his words. "What do you mean?"

He shrugged, glancing out the window as they headed farther into open water. "Someone once told me that we weren't put here on this earth to be happy. We were put on earth to make a difference. Sometimes those two things aren't one and the same."

"So, I'm being selfish pursuing my dreams of sailing rather than going to med school?" Confusion captured her voice.

"I didn't say that. Life is complicated. There's no right or wrong answer to that. You just need to listen to your gut. Besides, who says you can't make a difference on a charter boat?" *You can make a difference to me.* He said that last part silently, knowing better than to speak it aloud.

"You're right. I just have a lot of thinking to do." Kenzie let out a long sigh and stepped back. "I guess I need to get to work before Sunni finds me and fusses at me again."

Her words caused a weight to press on his chest. "If she gives you too hard of a time, let me know."

She offered a grateful smile. "I will. I'll talk to you later."

But as soon as Kenzie left the bridge, Jimmy James couldn't help but think she had taken a little piece of sunshine with her.

AS KENZIE LEFT the bridge and rounded the corner toward the main salon, she nearly collided with someone. She sucked in a breath and jerked back at the close call.

Sunni scowled back at her.

How long had the chief stew been standing there? Had she overheard any of Kenzie's conversation with the captain? The door had been closed, so that shouldn't be the case. Still, Kenzie felt uneasy.

Sunni narrowed her eyes, not bothering to hide her scrutiny. "Is everything okay?"

"It's fine. Why?"

"Because usually people don't talk to the captain unless they're having issues. Is there anything you want to say to me?"

Kenzie squared her shoulders, deciding not to play this game with her. "If I had something to say to you, I would say it."

"Good." Sunni crossed her arms. "So, if you weren't in there talking about me, what were you doing?"

Kenzie stared at Sunni, not breaking their gaze. "That's none of your business."

Satisfaction glimmered in Sunni's eyes. "You were flirting with the captain, weren't you?"

Kenzie felt her nostrils flare. "No, as a matter of fact, I wasn't."

"I see the way the two of you look at each other. You're not tricking anyone."

"I'm not trying to trick anyone, but thanks for the opinion." Kenzie tried to push past Sunni when the woman grabbed her arm. "This isn't your world."

Kenzie bristled at the demeaning sound of Sunni's tone. "What are you talking about?"

"Working on the crew. You're more of the type to come here because your family chartered a boat like this than you are the type to work on a boat like this."

Kenzie jerked out of her grasp before hissing, "You don't know me."

Sunni's gaze hardened. "But I do. I've been doing this job for three years now, and I've seen uncountable women just like you here on these boats. They've all failed. One of them even died."

Kenzie sucked in a breath at her unexpected statement. "What?"

"She didn't know what she was doing and fell overboard as the boat was being docked. She was crushed."

"That's terrible."

"Don't let that be you."

If Kenzie's gaze could burn into someone, Sunni would be on fire right now. "Is that a threat?"

Sunni snorted. "Of course not. It's my way of saying I care."

Kenzie felt the irritation rising in her. But, instead of lashing out, she muttered, "I need to go."

But just as she stepped away, Owen came down the hallway, his eyes crinkling in curiosity as he paused in front of them. "Have you guys seen Chef Durango lately?"

Another surge of concern rushed through Kenzie. "Not lately. Why?"

"He seemed distracted this morning. He almost cut off his finger while chopping some nuts for the top of the parfaits. I figured it was because of Waldo. Anyway, we've got to start getting things ready for lunch, and I can't find him anywhere."

Kenzie's heart beat harder. She hoped Durango hadn't disappeared like Waldo. The thought, on an ordinary day, would be an overreaction. But, given everything that had happened, no one on this boat could afford to let down their guard.

She and Sunni glanced at each other, and for a moment the two were on the same page.

Sunni stepped back, looking ready to spring into action. "I'll take the top deck if you take the bottom."

Kenzie nodded, hoping this didn't end with another crisis.

CHAPTER SEVENTEEN

JIMMY JAMES HEARD people scurrying on the deck and wondered if they were getting ready for lunch or if they were having another argument.

He started to radio Eddie for an update when his phone rang again. This time it was Police Chief Chambers. He'd also called her earlier and left a message.

He'd figure out the source of the commotion in a minute. Right now, he wanted to talk to the chief. For privacy, he closed the door and remained on the bridge.

"Hey, Jimmy James. How's the cruise going?"

He walked toward the window and stared out over the water as he filled her in on the situation with Waldo.

When he finished, the chief clucked her tongue. "His disappearance does sound suspicious. But I don't blame you for leaving—especially if someone saw this guy walk off the boat of his own free will. Hopefully, the police in Virginia Beach will keep their eyes on that situation."

"That's what I'm hoping also." He leaned against the window and let out a long breath.

"How's everything else going?" Chief Chambers asked.

"The whole situation with Captain Bridgemore has me on edge."

"Understandably."

"I know you probably can't tell me much, but I wondered if there were any new developments you're able to share. I'm concerned about the crew and want to make sure everyone is safe."

"Normally, I can't share details," Chief Chambers said. "But there *is* one thing I can tell you. We found the murder weapon."

His back straightened at the unexpected news. "What?"

"We sent some divers down with metal detectors to test my theory that the weapon had been thrown in the water. We're testing it now, but we feel confident that whoever killed the captain tossed this knife into the harbor thinking we'd never recover it."

A spark of hope flitted to life inside him. Maybe the knife would provide some answers. "Anything special about it?"

"It has a wooden handle with a wavy design. It's actually pretty unique."

Jimmy James pressed his lips together as he tried to picture it. "Does it look like something a fisherman might use?"

"That's what we're trying to figure out. Would you mind if I sent you a picture of it? Since you work down at the docks, maybe you've seen someone with it."

"I'd be more than happy to help if I can. Send it my way."

"I'll do that. And in the meantime, please be careful. Until we know what's going on, assume the worst."

"Don't worry, I have been." He frowned, not liking the sound of that.

A moment later, Chief Chambers sent him the photo of the knife.

Jimmy James called Siv to take over at the helm. Then, just to satisfy his curiosity, he headed to the galley.

He'd seen a knife like the one in the photograph before. But where?

When he stepped into the space, he noticed the kitchen was empty. The scent of bacon and butter filled the air.

Where was Chef Durango? He should be preparing lunch. Late food made for unhappy guests. Bread was laid out as well as lunchmeat and cheese. It looked like Chef Durango had been preparing to make paninis but had stopped halfway through.

Jimmy James paused by a kitchen drawer and opened it.

He sucked in a breath when he saw the cutlery inside.

It was a set of knives . . . and the handles on them matched the handle of the one in the picture Cassidy had sent.

Just as Jimmy James picked up a knife to examine it more, a shadow appeared in the doorway.

He looked up and saw Chef Durango staring at him, a startled look in his eyes.

"WHAT ARE you doing with my knife?" Chef Durango's gaze shifted to the knife in Jimmy James' hand. The man appeared stiff, and his gaze didn't look as focused as normal.

Jimmy James cautiously stepped closer, determined to get to the heart of the matter. "The bigger question is why one of your knives was used to murder Captain Bridgemore."

Durango's eyes widened, and he let out a light gasp. "What are you talking about?"

"When did you get to Lantern Beach, Durango?"

The chef pressed his lips together in a tight line. "Why's it matter?"

"Just answer the question."

He let out a long breath. "I got into town a day earlier, okay? But that doesn't mean anything."

"Unfortunately, that means you were on Lantern Beach at the same time the captain was murdered. Now a knife from your personal collection was found and identified as the murder weapon. Care to explain yourself?"

Durango manically shook his head and stepped back, almost as if he wanted to flee. "I don't know what you're talking about. I didn't do anything to the captain."

"Did you know Captain Bridgemore before you

came on this trip?" Jimmy James braced himself, uncertain if Durango would lash out or run. He needed to be prepared for either.

"I worked with him one time on a two-day cruise. That's it." Chef Durango sliced his hand through the air as if to add finality to his statement. "We didn't have any problems with each other. None!"

Jimmy James crossed his arms, not ready for this conversation to be done. "Something isn't adding up here, Durango. What's going on? Why do you look so ill at ease?"

"I started to feel a little sick, and everyone started panicking, looking all over the boat for me. Everything that's happened has shaken them, and they thought I was missing."

"But I guess they found you?"

He nodded. "Owen did. He told the others so they wouldn't worry."

"Why did you feel sick? Was it something you ate?"

"I don't think so." His hand went to his stomach. "I think I'm having some seasickness, but I don't know why. I've never had it before."

Nausea could explain the strange look in his eyes. Jimmy James had known of people who'd had strange bouts of seasickness that seemed to pop up at random times, so he couldn't rule out the possibility that his chef was telling the truth.

He hoped the opposite wasn't true. Could the chef be feeling like this because someone had slipped him something?

Jimmy James had no reason to think so. But he wanted to keep an eye on Durango, just in case.

In the meantime, he still had more questions.

"How about your knife?" Jimmy James held one up, careful not to do so in a threatening manner. "If you're not the one who killed Captain Bridgemore, how did somebody else get something that belongs to you?"

Chef Durango swiped a hand through his hair. "I wish I could tell you. But when I arrived in Lantern Beach, I left everything I'd brought with me in the back of my car. I parked at the harbor and slept in my car that night."

Jimmy James listened, trying to reserve his opinion. "And the next day?"

Durango let out a long breath. "If you must know, the next day, I went to the beach for a few hours before everyone else arrived. I was flirting with one of the lifeguards there. I can't tell you her name, but I can describe her. Certainly, somebody in town knows who she is."

Jimmy James eyed him, knowing how important it was to get to the truth. The safety of everyone on the boat depended on it. "So, you think someone just happened to find the knives in your car and grabbed one right before he or she murdered the captain?"

Chef Durango sagged against the door, looking as if another wave of seasickness was coming over him. "I know how it sounds, but I left my car unlocked. I always do. Those knives were in the backseat along with some of my other kitchen equipment. I did notice one of them was missing when I unpacked them, but I never thought it was because someone used it as a murder weapon."

Jimmy James stared at Durango another moment, trying to figure out if he believed him or not.

His gut told him that someone wasn't telling the truth on this boat.

The question was, who?

CHAPTER EIGHTEEN

KENZIE FELT the tension in the air as Jimmy James called the crew in for another meeting on the bridge.

They all stood anxiously in a semicircle as they waited to hear what he had to say. Clearly, there was an update of some sort. She had a feeling Jimmy James had bad news.

The captain stood at the front of the room, the water and the sky blurring into a smear of blue behind him as Siv stood at the helm, monitoring the waterways.

"I think you all know there have been some suspicious things going on, and we need to clear the air right now," Jimmy James started.

"I started to walk into the galley, and I overheard

your conversations there," Eddie blurted. "Did Durango kill Captain Bridgemore?"

"I didn't kill anybody." An edge of defensiveness cut through Durango's voice as he stood back from the rest of the group.

Jimmy James raised a hand, indicating they should quiet. "Let's not throw out accusations. Let's talk facts instead. Captain Bridgemore was stabbed. The murder weapon was found, and the knife matches a set of knives belonging to Durango."

Kenzie felt herself recoil at that update.

Everyone else must have felt the same because a murmur rippled through the group.

Chef Durango? Was he capable of murder? He seemed like such a kind, creative soul.

Now that she thought about it, the whole time the crew was looking for Waldo, Durango was nowhere to be seen.

She stored that fact in the back of her mind.

"*However*," Jimmy James continued, his voice pointed. "I called and verified his alibi. Chef Durango was at the beach during the time of the murder. Most likely, the killer grabbed a knife from Durango's car before killing Captain Bridgemore. That fact also makes his death a premeditated murder because if someone grabbed a knife before-hand, then the altercation was clearly planned."

Kenzie frowned. That didn't make her feel any better.

In fact, a chill washed over her at the thought.

"We also know that Waldo is missing." Jimmy James began pacing in front of them, almost reminding Kenzie of a lawyer at trial. "There's a good chance he left on his own, but there's also a chance he did not."

He paused, and silence stretched throughout the room.

Kenzie had a feeling no one knew what to say. Everyone was still trying to process this news.

Finally, Jimmy James spoke again. "Needless to say, we all need to be on guard right now until the police figure out what's going on."

"Is it even safe for us to be on this trip?" Sunni's voice cracked as if she were truly scared. Her eyes were wide, and her actions seemed stiff with fear.

Eddie moved closer to her, as if he wanted to comfort her. But he didn't dare touch her in front of the rest of the group.

"The moment I see any indication that it's not safe for us to be on this trip, I'm calling it off," Jimmy

James said. "I'm not willing to risk anybody's life just so we can get a paycheck."

Silence hung in the air again. As it did, Jimmy James scanned the face of each person in the room.

Kenzie felt her cheeks heat when he looked at her. Did he think she had something to do with this? Why did that possibility make her feel a surge of disappointment?

"Before we conclude this meeting, does anybody have anything that they want to share?" Jimmy James asked.

No one said anything.

The captain slowly nodded. "Very well then. But if anyone knows anything about this, I need you to talk to me. Now, in a few minutes we'll be pulling into Cape Charles. Buster hasn't made it clear what his plans are once he gets there. He likes to play things by ear, as he says. So, we all need to be ready for whatever his requests are."

"He's a jerk." Sunni rolled her eyes to the side as she crossed her arms.

Jimmy James' stern gaze stopped on her. "Yes, but he's also our guest. We only have two more days until we drop this group off. Let's see if we can get through them. Are you all with me?"

Everyone nodded, although no one seemed especially enthusiastic.

Kenzie flooded out with the rest of the crew. The way Jimmy James had handled the meeting was impressive. This couldn't be easy on him, but he'd handled it firmly yet with compassion.

But the more time that passed, the more certain she was that trouble was still lingering too close for comfort.

JIMMY JAMES PULLED into the harbor of Cape Charles, Virginia, a quaint town located on the Chesapeake Bay. Thankfully, the marina contained a slip big and deep enough to accommodate this vessel.

From here, the guests could get off the boat and walk to the little town. The problem was, Jimmy James didn't see Buster as being the type to enjoy a picturesque area. So exactly where was his mind right now?

The captain headed to the table where lunch was wrapping up to address the passengers, trying to put on his best face as he did so.

But he'd noticed a new somberness in the group

since Waldo disappeared.

"I'd like to welcome you to Cape Charles, Virginia," Jimmy James started. "I think you'll find it's a great town. What are you guys thinking about doing while you're here?"

"I thought I might hang out on the boat for a while." Buster raised his chin as he lounged back on a deck chair with a drink in hand.

Something about his actions and the way he said the words made Jimmy James think that the guy was on edge. Buster was trying to make it seem like it wasn't a big deal that Waldo had left. But Jimmy James had a feeling that it was—especially if Buster couldn't upload his stunt videos.

Had Waldo's departure been a blow to Buster's ego, and now he wanted to push back and prove that he was okay without his friend?

"We can pull out the Jet Skis and Seabobs, and you guys could just have fun out here in the bay," Jimmy James suggested. "It's going to be a beautiful day. High of eighty-five, wind is eight knots, and low humidity. We don't get a lot of days like this in the South."

"That sounds great," Buster said. "That's what we'll do. Is everybody good with that?"

Everyone around him nodded.

"Okay, then we'll get those ready for you," Jimmy James said. "If you have any special requests for dinner, please let us know that as well."

"Will do." Buster rose and clamped Jimmy James' arm. "Those are some serious guns. You ex-military?"

Jimmy James felt his jaw tighten. He hoped this guy didn't ask too many questions about his past. While he usually didn't mind talking about it, he wasn't sure how comfortable his guests would feel if they knew too many details.

"No, not military," he finally said.

"I should have guessed. You're too much of a bad boy for that, aren't you?" Buster studied his expression for another moment. "Motorcycle gang?"

Jimmy James shook his head again. "No motorcycle gang."

Buster stared at him before smiling and nodding. "I'll figure you out sometime. When I do, maybe we can even do a YouTube video together."

"Maybe," he answered, careful to remain noncommittal.

Jimmy James didn't like the thought of Buster trying to get too close. Because if anybody started digging into his past then his future in boating might be ruined.

CHAPTER NINETEEN

AS KENZIE FINISHED a sandwich in the crew galley, her phone rang. Her heart skipped a beat when she saw her father was calling. He hadn't called her in a month—not since her last semester ended and she told him she wasn't going back. So why was he trying to get in touch now?

Her hands trembled as she put her phone to her ear. "Hello?"

"Mackenzie? Is that you?" Her father's voice wasn't as warm and jovial as it had once been. Too many things had happened for him to keep that joy in his tone.

She wandered from the galley to the deck at the stern of the boat, which was empty. She leaned against the railing as she braced herself for whatever this conversation might hold.

"It's me," she said. "I wasn't expecting to hear from you."

"Leesa just showed me a video of you online." Outrage tinged his voice. "You're on that Buster guy's YouTube account singing karaoke, and not well, I might add. What in the world is going on? Have you lost your mind?"

She glanced around to make sure no one was close by as dread filled her stomach. "I told you I was going to take a job on a charter boat. That's what I did."

"Kenzie . . . you have so much more to offer than this." His disappointment was clear.

Guilt filled her, as it always did when she let her father down.

She remembered what Jimmy James had said earlier about how life wasn't about our happiness. Had he been implying that she should give up her own desires in order to pursue a medical degree?

Kenzie wasn't sure. Even though Jimmy James had given her something to think about, his words weren't enough to change her mind. Nor were her father's.

Some people might call her stubborn. She thought she simply knew what she wanted.

"I just needed a break," she told him. "The pressure was getting to me, and—"

"Medical school is a great opportunity to learn how to deal with that pressure. You think it's bad in school? Just wait until you get into the operating room."

"Dad . . . I don't want to have this discussion with you again." Every time Kenzie did, it hadn't turned out well.

The tension of this conversation added to the tension she already felt because of what was happening on the boat. She reminded herself to take several deep breaths to control her stress.

"I don't want you on that boat." He said the words as if they were an order. "Come home. Let's talk."

She let out a sigh. "We tried that. There's nothing to say. It's only me trying to see things your way. That isn't a two-way street."

"Mackenzie . . ." his voice softened.

"Look, Dad. I love you. I really do. But it's clear that you can't have Leesa in your life and me. The mix between the two of us is just toxic. I'm going to make it easier for you. I'm not going to make you choose."

"Mackenzie . . . that's not what I want."

She frowned and lifted her head as the breeze swept over her face, seeming to remind her that a shift in the wind wasn't always a bad thing.

"I know, Dad. But I've already caused you enough strain." Her voice cracked as she said the words, "I love you."

Before he could say anything else, she ended the call. Tears wanted to fall from her eyes as the conversation weighed on her.

Her dad couldn't see that Leesa wanted him all to herself. Nothing would change that.

But Leesa also made her dad happy. Who was Kenzie to take that away from him?

There didn't seem to be a win-win in this situation. If Kenzie's mother was still alive, she would have gone to bat for Kenzie. Would have told her to pursue her dreams.

But her mom was gone, and now Kenzie only had her gut to follow . . . her gut, the memory of her mother's wisdom, and lots of prayers.

As she lifted her head, she heard a commotion in the distance.

What was going on?

She started toward the bow so she could find out.

"I'M GOING to need you to get down from up there," Jimmy James called.

"I don't want to." Buster stretched his arms above his head as if about to do a swan dive into the water below. "I paid for the cruise, and I can do what I want."

Irritation clawed at Jimmy James' muscles, and he had to rely on every ounce of his self-control right now. This would be the real test as to whether or not he had the finesse to be a captain on a boat like this.

"You did pay for this cruise, and we've done our best to accommodate you," he said, keeping his voice even. "But when it comes to matters of safety, I'm afraid I have to put my foot down."

That sounded firm but gentle, right? Trying to be diplomatic definitely wasn't his strength. Jimmy James liked to call things the way he saw them.

He stared at the twenty-one-year-old who stood on top of the boat, prepared to jump into the water below. Nikki recorded everything on her camera, and everyone else stood around watching.

Buster stared down at the water and shook his head. "I'm not going to get hurt, man."

"You don't know that," Jimmy James said. "You could hit the deck on the way down. Too many things can go wrong."

"I'm going to do it anyway." Buster scooted closer to the edge as if he was about to jump.

Another round of exasperation rushed through Jimmy James. This guy was a punk. There was no other way to say it.

He drew in a deep breath before speaking again. "I'm going to give you to the count of three to get down. Otherwise, the charter will be over."

"You'd cancel my trip because *I'm* trying to jump off a boat that *I* rented?"

"That's right. Even though you paid a lot of money for this charter, there are still rules in place. I wish you hadn't put me in this position." Jimmy James continued to stare at the top deck, squinting against the bright sun.

He was strangely aware of everyone around them —both the crew and the guests.

And Kenzie.

Maybe *especially* Kenzie.

Everybody watched right now to see how the situation would play out.

Jimmy James had a feeling he'd be starring in this guy's next video. The thought made his blood go hot. If this went south . . . being caught on video would be a very bad thing.

"You're pretty uptight sometimes, man." Buster lowered his arms and stared down at Jimmy James.

Uptight wasn't something people usually called Jimmy James. In fact, at one time he'd been the life of the party. But sometimes with responsibility came a shift from being carefree to being more serious.

Too many tragedies had already occurred in the past several days. He wasn't going to add another one to the list.

Jimmy James stared at Buster and waited for him to make his decision. He feared that at any moment this guy might just jump from the top deck to spite him. Jimmy James wouldn't put it past him.

Finally, Buster raised his hands in surrender. "Okay, fine. I'll get down. But I need another idea for one of my stunts."

Jimmy James' thoughts raced as he tried to come up with something that might appease the extrovert.

That's when Eddie stepped up. "I've been to this harbor before. Some of the old houses have widow's walks. I'm sure you could come up with some stunts that might take place there—if an owner will give you access. There are also some sand cliffs a little farther down that could make for some interesting footage."

Buster stared at him for a moment before nodding. "I like the way you think. I think I *will* check out some of those widow's walks."

Jimmy James released the air from his lungs. One problem solved. But he was far from being able to relax yet.

"What about dinner?" Jimmy James asked. "Do you have any preferences?"

"I'd like something nice. But early. Maybe at five. I want it to be fancy. Six courses. Can we do that? Oh, and I want some of the crew to join me." A sparkle lit his eyes.

"We don't normally join our guests—"

"I insist." He clapped his hands in the air as if demanding attention. "Can we make this happen? Chop chop?"

Irritation climbed his spine at Buster's words. Jimmy James considered what to say for a moment before finally nodding. "We'll make it happen."

But he couldn't help but think this guy had something else up his sleeve. The question was, what?

CHAPTER TWENTY

CHEF DURANGO HAD BEEN in a tizzy ever since he'd heard Buster wanted an early six-course dinner tonight with the crew. Kenzie didn't even try to keep up with everything Durango muttered as he ran around the kitchen.

Sunni had disappeared, trying to come up with some type of table decoration to make the dining area look "fancy" as Buster had requested. Kenzie had been charged with cutting up some vegetables.

As Durango began to prepare some beef Wellington, he glanced at Kenzie. "So, I heard Eddie and Sunni talking today."

Kenzie's gut squeezed with dread as she anticipated where this conversation might go. There was no telling what those two had said.

"Is that right?" she finally asked, carefully slicing an onion to Durango's exacting standards.

"They were talking about Captain Gamble. Saying how he's done time."

This didn't come as a surprise to Kenzie, but she kept chopping, trying not to show any trepidation. "People change."

Durango glanced back at her, disdain in his gaze. "I guess they do. But, considering everything that's going on, maybe our captain should be our most likely suspect."

"Jimmy James? I mean, Captain Gamble?" Kenzie said his name with a wispy laugh. "He couldn't hurt a fly."

Durango paused, grabbed a sharpener, and began to work on his knife blade. "Are you sure he didn't go to jail for assault?"

"No . . . he went to jail for some petty crimes." Her throat tightened as she watched the chef, as she realized just how sharp that knife would be when Durango finished.

She remembered hearing him talk without an accent. Maybe he was trying to deflect right now, to make other people look suspicious.

Durango raised an eyebrow. "Is that what he told you?"

Kenzie sliced the onion with a little more force than necessary. "Do you know something different or is this just conjecture?"

He shrugged and put down the sharpener. "I'm just saying that this guy isn't going to admit if he went there for some type of violent act. But it wouldn't surprise me. He seems like the type. Did you see his tats? Not all tats are for fun. Some have meaning."

Kenzie swallowed hard. She wouldn't believe that Jimmy James could be violent. She wanted to believe the best of him and wouldn't let Durango plant any doubt in her mind.

"I've got to get ready for dinner," she said instead.

Durango shrugged.

She stepped away but paused, tired of tiptoeing around the truth. "Chef Durango, why did I overhear you talking without an accent the other day?"

His eyes widened. "What? I don't know what you're talking about."

"I think you do," she said. "You're faking your accent. What are *you* hiding?"

He quickly shook his head and backed away. "Nothing. I'm not hiding anything."

"I don't believe you." Kenzie crossed her arms.

Finally, Durango let out a sigh. "Look, you're right. I don't always have an accent."

As he said the words, his accent disappeared.

"What does that mean?" Kenzie asked.

He sighed again. "I think people take me more seriously if they think I have an accent. It makes me seem legit."

"Really?"

"What?" He shrugged, his voice climbing. "My mom is French. I may be faking the accent, but that's the only reason I'm doing it. It's not because I'm trying to hide who I really am or because I'm secretly a criminal."

Durango stared at her, as if waiting for confirmation she believed him.

But Kenzie couldn't give that to him. Not yet.

One thing was for sure, she had a lot to think about.

———

JIMMY JAMES SUCKED in a breath when he saw Kenzie walk onto the deck for dinner that evening wearing a slim-fitting black dress.

She had curves in all the right places. She'd

pulled her hair back into a twist, skillfully applied makeup, and looked like a million bucks.

He stood when he saw her, hoping his rush of attraction didn't show all over his features.

"Don't you look nice, Kenzie." Buster beat him to the punch as their guest cast her an approving look.

She smiled as she took a seat across the table from Jimmy James. "Thank you."

One of the outside tables had been set up for this evening's festivities. It was the perfect temperate day for outdoor dining. The breeze felt balmy, the waves lapped gently, and the humidity had lifted. Soft music played in the background, and everyone was dressed to the nines.

Eddie and Owen had agreed to serve tonight so Sunni and Kenzie would be able to eat with the guests. Buster appeared to like the company of pretty women, even when his girlfriend Nikki was around.

What did that say about the man's character? Nothing good from Jimmy James' perspective.

Jimmy James felt like he could hardly swallow as he glanced across the table at Kenzie. He had to stop looking at her, but it was hard to pull his eyes away. She looked absolutely gorgeous.

"How did your stunt go today?" Kenzie glanced at Buster.

His face lit with excitement. "It was great. I made it look like I was running straight off the edge of a widow's walk. The power of special effects. Great idea, Eddie." Buster smiled at Eddie as the bosun refilled water goblets on the table.

"No problem."

Jimmy James could tell by Eddie's expression that he didn't appreciate having to work as a server tonight. But Buster had specifically mentioned whom he wanted at dinner and whom he wanted to serve.

He glanced across the table and saw Buster's mom had a far-off look in her eyes. He had to wonder if the woman was on antidepressants, based on her mellow behavior. As usual, she touched the necklace at her throat as she stared into the distance.

What was behind her gaze? Did she ever wish she could go back to the simple days when her family hadn't had money? When maybe her son hadn't been so full of himself?

Everyone always thought money would solve their problems when in fact money usually just created more issues. Different issues.

Not like he would know. Jimmy James had never

had a lot of money. Based on the way this charter was going, that wouldn't be changing anytime soon. Most likely, he'd remain stuck being a dockhand for the rest of his life.

The thought pressed heavily on him.

He stood, suddenly needing a deep breath. He muttered an excuse about checking something on the bridge and then excused himself for a minute.

But as he walked past the main salon, he spotted Gilbert and Nikki inside. They'd slipped away from dinner—Gilbert to take a phone call and Nikki to run to the restroom.

Instead, the two of them whispered to each other.

What was that about?

He didn't know, but he stored his suspicions in the back of his mind. With everything that had happened, he couldn't afford to let his guard down.

CHAPTER TWENTY-ONE

AS KENZIE PICKED at her roasted potatoes, she couldn't help but think that Jimmy James wasn't acting like himself.

Durango's words came back to her—his suspicion that the captain might be somehow involved in the recent crimes surrounding the boat.

Could Durango's misgivings be accurate? Or was the captain acting strangely for some other reason?

From the moment Jimmy James had seen Kenzie walk toward the dinner table, something on his face had changed.

Should she have worn a different outfit? Maybe this one wasn't appropriate.

She wasn't sure, and she tried not to feel self-conscious about it.

Unlike Sunni.

Kenzie wasn't sure if that woman ever felt self-conscious a day in her life. Right now, she giggled before stabbing a piece of steak and taking a bite.

Kenzie had never been the type to use people. But her impression of Sunni left her feeling like that was exactly the kind of person Sunni was. When Sunni saw an opportunity, the woman did whatever was necessary to make sure it happened.

She still wondered if Sunni had taken her earrings just to play with her mind. She made the most sense.

But Kenzie had a lot of theories and no real evidence.

As dinner ended, Buster stood. "I'm going to explore the area this evening with my family and friends. Maybe do a nighttime hike or find a good club. Either way, we won't be needing any of your assistance, so feel free to take the evening off."

The crew glanced at each other, wondering if it was too good to be true.

"I mean it." Buster's gaze traveled across the table, locking with each of the crew members. "You guys have been working hard, and I'm not exactly easy to get along with all the time. So, take the night off. Go get dessert together or something to drink or take a nap. We'll be fine for the rest of the day. I just have one request. Sunni, could you watch Laney?"

Sunni's smile faded before a fake, less enthusiastic one appeared. "Of course."

Jimmy James stood, his arms stiff and his expression professional. "Would you like for us to arrange transportation for you?"

"That's a good idea," Buster said.

Kenzie nibbled on the inside of her lip. Was this truly a generous offer? Or was Buster trying to get rid of any possible supervision—or voices of reason —because of an ulterior motive?

"We'll get things ready for your departure," Jimmy James said.

Kenzie couldn't be sure. But she remained cautiously optimistic that maybe she'd have some time to relax this evening. That sounded like exactly what the doctor ordered.

———

JIMMY JAMES KNEW he shouldn't do it. But he did it anyway.

As he saw Kenzie step down the gangplank, he called after her. She paused and turned to him. Her gaze lit when she saw it was him.

"Do you mind if I walk with you?" He asked partly because he was worried about her and partly because he wanted to get to know this woman more.

"I would be honored, Captain."

He increased his strides and quickly caught up with her, surprised by how self-conscious he felt when she said his title like that. "How about for just a night you call me Jimmy James."

"Fine. Jimmy James then." She flashed a grin.

She strolled beside him, still wearing that black dress that looked killer on her. The aroma of her perfume drifted toward him, something flowery and subtle. Something that made him want to lean closer so he could inhale it more deeply—not that he would do that. But it was tempting.

"What are your plans for your night off?" He tried to sound casual even though part of him felt like a prepubescent boy who had a crush on the prettiest girl in class.

"I have no idea. But I've never been to Cape Charles, and I thought it might be fun to explore."

"I came here once, but I was on a fishing trip. I've heard great things about it."

They crossed down the sidewalk from the harbor and headed toward the downtown area. The scent of salty water lingered in the air, along with the aroma of fresh coffee and fried seafood.

She glanced up at Jimmy James, nothing but kindness in her gaze. "Do you like to travel?"

He shrugged as he thought about his answer. He felt like he should say something that made him sound cultured and sophisticated. But, if he did, he'd be lying.

"I don't know," he admitted. "I've never really had the opportunity to travel, other than on fishing trips. Most of them have been off the coast of Carolina or Virginia, though."

"It seems like being on a boat has been your whole life."

"I guess in some ways it has. Boats are where I feel most at home."

"They're a good place to feel at home."

He smiled. He liked the sound of that—although the trips he'd been on weren't probably anything like Kenzie envisioned. They were filled with fish guts and sweltering sun and backbreaking work.

He wouldn't have it any other way.

He nodded at a coffeehouse in the distance. "What do you say? You want to get something to drink?"

She glanced up at him, a playful smile on her

face. "Are you allowed to socialize with me, one of the little people?"

"I would never consider you a little person. So, I'm going to make an executive decision on that and say yes."

Her grin widened. "In that case, I would love to."

Warmth spread through him at the idea of spending more time with her. The rest of the crew had probably gone out looking for a bar. But Kenzie didn't seem like that type, and Jimmy James stayed away from alcohol, especially considering his past.

He placed his hand on the small of her back and led her inside the shop.

He was looking forward to this evening more than he'd looked forward to anything in a long time.

CHAPTER TWENTY-TWO

KENZIE HAD ALMOST SAID no to walking with Jimmy James—mostly because Durango's words kept replaying in her head. She'd always been more of a dreamer and less of a realist. Her father had chided her for her optimism. Had told her she was too trusting.

She didn't want to put herself in a bad situation now, one where her naivety put her in danger.

However, she knew Jimmy James was like a big teddy bear who looked tough on the outside but who was warm and gooey on the inside—unless somebody was in danger. Then his personality could flip. But that wasn't necessarily a bad thing.

She took another sip of her vanilla latte, realizing

how much she had missed these. Then she turned to Jimmy James, questions racing through her head.

"Can I ask you something?" She ran her finger down the ceramic handle of her coffee mug as she contemplated her words.

Trepidation spread across his features, and she realized he probably didn't want to divulge too much about his past. She could understand that. But that didn't mean she couldn't dig deeper.

"Shoot," he said.

She tilted her head, trying to make her question sound more casual than it probably was. "Have you ever been in love before?"

His eyes widened as if he hadn't expected the question.

"As a matter of fact, yes. I have been in love once before." He nodded slowly. "I dated a girl named Lucy back in high school."

"What happened with Lucy?"

A shadow seemed to fall over his gaze, and she instantly regretted asking.

"You don't have to—"

"No, it's okay," Jimmy James insisted. "I just haven't talked about her in a while." He stared at his cup for a moment as if gathering his thoughts. "Honestly, I thought the two of us would end up getting married one day. But that's when I started getting into some trouble, and she dumped me. I couldn't blame her. But for a while I held onto hope that maybe I would be able to win her back."

"Did you?"

"For a while." The shadow across his gaze deepened. "But I made some stupid mistakes."

Kenzie sucked in a breath. "Was she the one . . . ?" She couldn't finish the statement.

Jimmy James nodded. "She was the one who almost died because I couldn't get her help when I was high."

"I'm so sorry. I shouldn't have—"

He raised his hand. "No, it's okay."

She gave him a look.

"Really," he insisted.

Kenzie remained quiet a moment to give him time to direct the conversation away from this subject or to explain more. She was fine with either.

"She fell off a ladder and hit her head," he started, his voice notably more somber. "She was unconscious when I found her. I knew I couldn't drive. But I couldn't find my phone either. I couldn't think straight."

"What happened?"

"I went to the neighbors, and they helped. But

still . . ." He let out a deep breath. "Anyway, today she's married with two kids, and she seems really happy. She moved away from Lantern Beach, farther up north toward the Nags Head area. We still keep up with each other on occasion."

"That's good," Kenzie said. "I'm glad everything turned out okay."

She could only imagine how he might have beaten himself up for that. Thankfully, he had a happy ending and seemed to have learned from his mistakes.

Jimmy James' eyes studied Kenzie in a way that might have made her uncomfortable with some people—but not with him.

"What about you?" he asked softly. "Have you ever been in a serious relationship?"

The inquiry shouldn't have caught her by surprise. It was natural that he'd turn the question back to her. Still, she fluttered around in her thoughts trying to figure out what to say.

She took a sip of her coffee before placing her mug back on the table. "Actually, I haven't. I've never been in a really serious relationship, and I've definitely never been in love."

He raised his eyebrows. "Really? That's not what I thought you would say."

She shrugged, feeling more self-conscious about it than she would have liked. "Sometimes, I feel like I must be a loser if I've never been in love. But I've just never met the right person, and I don't want to force something that's not real."

"That definitely doesn't make you a loser."

She shrugged. "It's just that I'm twenty-five years old. Most people my age have been in love at least once. But it seems like all the guys who've asked me out are so boring. I just haven't felt that spark I'm looking for."

He stabbed his straw into his blended coffee drink. "You're looking for a spark, huh?"

She lifted one shoulder and then the other as she tried to work out her thoughts. "Yeah, I guess I am. I mean, I'd want to be really great friends with whoever I fell in love with. But there still needs to be that spark, that chemistry. Don't you think?"

He grinned. "I do think that's important."

She let out a little laugh. "I don't know why I'm telling you all this. It's not something I talk about very often."

"It's good to hear you talk and open up. You're a very interesting girl, Kenzie Anderson."

She twisted her neck. "And I think you're a very

interesting guy, Jimmy James. I feel like you're a book of secrets that's just waiting to be unlocked."

He let out a chuckle. "I don't think I've ever been described like that before."

"Well, now you have."

The two of them exchanged glances, and Kenzie felt a surge of happiness like she hadn't experienced in a long time.

Jimmy James was so unlikely as someone she should feel this connection with. But she did. However, she had no idea what to do about it.

"YOU FEEL like stretching your legs a little bit?" Kenzie looked up at Jimmy James and waited for his response. She needed to walk off some of the calories she'd consumed tonight at that six-course meal. The sugary coffee drink probably hadn't helped, but the time off the boat had been worth it.

Jimmy James flashed a grin. "With you? I'd love to."

Her cheeks warmed at his words. She didn't want this man to have this effect on her. But he did. No amount of denying it would change that.

At that thought, she remembered what Sunni

had told her. *I see the way the two of you look at each other. You're not tricking anyone.*

There was no merit in the woman's words. Kenzie would be smart to simply brush them off and move on. She and Jimmy James . . . did they really have anything in common? Certainly, their pasts were different.

Yet, at the same time, he was full of surprises. She'd expected him to be all muscle and brawn. But he was also smart, and his leadership skills couldn't be denied.

The two of them stepped from the coffee shop into the balmy air. Even though it was summertime, the evening felt pleasant right now. In fact, almost everything about their little excursion tonight had felt pretty perfect.

She glanced over at him as they strolled beside each other. "Do you see yourself staying in Lantern Beach for a long time?"

He shrugged, his hands in his pockets. "I don't really know. I love the island and the people there. But sometimes I think it would be good to get a fresh start."

"It does seem like a nice place, despite all the bad things that happened since I arrived."

He nodded. "You were definitely given a baptism by fire."

They reached the end of the downtown area and began sauntering toward a dock that led out over the Chesapeake Bay. Surprisingly few people were out here tonight, considering the beautiful weather. But she wasn't complaining.

They paused halfway down the boardwalk, and Kenzie leaned against one of the railings, looking out over the water as the moon shone above it. The sight was so peaceful.

Jimmy James paused beside her. "What are you thinking?"

"You really want to know?" She raised an eyebrow.

"I wouldn't have asked if I didn't."

"Part of me dreads being on this boat anymore," she admitted. "I guess there's a part of me that just wants to go back to the safety of my old life. But that's not a possibility."

"Change can be hard."

"In so many ways, I feel like I've run aground just like a boat might," she continued. "I feel like I was sailing in smooth waters when I suddenly hit a sandbar, and now everything needs to be recalculated."

"Good analogy. But even boats that have run aground can be set afloat again."

She glanced at him and flashed a grin. "Thank you. Listen, I just want to let you know that I think you're doing a great job as captain. I know you've had to make some hard calls, but you're doing great. I could see you doing this for a long time."

As he looked at her, his eyes widened as if her words had triggered something inside him.

"Not very many people have believed in me throughout my life," he said quietly.

Kenzie turned toward him, feeling the pressing need to offer some encouragement. "I believe in you."

As she said the words, their gazes caught, and something crackled between them. She felt it. She was certain Jimmy James did also.

She stared at his jaw. His ear. His lips. She wanted nothing more than to reach out and touch his cheek. To feel his five o'clock shadow against her fingertips. She wanted to know what it would be like to be in his arms. To inhale his soapy-clean scent.

Based on the way Jimmy James looked at her, he wanted the same. The connection between them was so strong it almost felt physical.

They weren't touching right now. So why did it feel like they were?

"Kenzie . . ." His voice sounded hoarse as he said her name.

"Yes?" Was she imagining things, or had she crept closer to him? She was treading in dangerous waters, but she couldn't seem to pull herself back to shore.

"You are . . ." Jimmy James' voice sounded hoarse as he stared at her.

The magnetism in his gaze made Kenzie unable to look away. In fact, all she wanted was to drink in this moment, to embrace the warmth filling her chest and lifting her spirits.

"Yes?" Her voice cracked as the word left her lips.

But before Jimmy James could finish his statement, someone shouted in the distance.

They both straightened and turned toward the sound.

They glanced over in time to see a man sprint across the road in front of a car. The driver yelled out the window. Meanwhile, the man ran down the sidewalk as if oblivious.

Jimmy James let out a grunt before muttering, "Stay here."

The next instant, he took off after the man.

CHAPTER TWENTY-THREE

JIMMY JAMES DIDN'T WANT to leave Kenzie behind.

But that looked like one of the men from the docks—and the same one he'd seen yesterday. What was he doing here now? Was this guy watching them? Or maybe even trying to keep an eye on *Almost Paradise*?

He needed to find out. This guy could hold the answers they'd been looking for, and Jimmy James couldn't let the opportunity slip away.

He ran down the dock and onto Main Street before skidding to a stop and glancing around. Where had the guy gone?

He thought he saw a shadow moving toward the

shops along Main Street. He sprinted in that direction, trying to watch his every step until he had his eyes on this guy.

As people glanced his way, Jimmy James slowed his steps. He didn't want to alarm anyone. Plus, moving more slowly allowed him to be more cautious.

As he walked past an alley, he spotted a figure running there.

It was the same guy. The man he was looking for.

The man turned and spotted him at the same time. He took off at a faster pace.

Jimmy James dashed toward the guy, thankful that he had longer legs that allowed him to easily close the distance between them. As soon as he was close enough, he grabbed the guy by the back of his shirt.

The man jerked to a halt. Without wasting any time, Jimmy James pushed him against the wall. Now it was time to get some answers.

"Who are you?" Jimmy James stared the guy dead square in the eye, not daring to look away and give this guy a chance to breathe. "And what are you doing?"

"Benjamin. My name is Benjamin." The scrappy

twenty-something raised his hands in the air. "I'm just taking a walk. Is something wrong with that?"

"If you were just taking a walk, why did you run?"

He shrugged. "I don't know, man. You're a big guy. You looked angry. Anyone in my shoes would run."

Jimmy James let out a little growl. "You and I both know that's not true. I've seen you before. At least at two different harbors—including Lantern Beach, where you hassled a friend of mine. Why are you following us?"

"I don't even know who you are." Benjamin's words came out fast and unsteady. "Why would I follow you?"

"That's what I'm trying to figure out. What are you doing in Cape Charles?"

Benjamin pulled his head back, almost as if trying to melt into the brick wall behind him. "Listen, buddy. You need to back off. I'm the first mate on a fishing charter that operates up and down the East Coast. If our paths have crossed it's only because it's a coincidence. Why would I follow you?"

He narrowed his eyes. "A fishing charter? Who's the captain?"

"Julius . . . Julius Smith."

Jimmy James had heard the name before. He thought he may have even met the man once.

"Where are you based out of?" Jimmy James continued.

"Wilmington."

"You remember giving my friend a hard time the other night in Lantern Beach?"

"It's kind of hard to forget about that."

"Where are the rest of your friends?"

Benjamin shook his head. "Not here."

Jimmy James narrowed his eyes. "There's something you're not telling me. Are you following Kenzie?"

"What? I—"

"Don't lie to me," Jimmy James warned him.

The man let out a sigh. "My friends are ticked off that our time with her was cut short. They told me to follow her. I wasn't going to do it, but then I saw her here, and I thought I might score some points with the guys. But that's it. I wasn't going to hurt her."

Jimmy James didn't feel confident of that.

"Now are you done with your questions?" Benjamin gave him a death glare.

Jimmy James continued to hold onto his shirt, not willing to risk this guy getting away. He didn't trust him as far as he could throw him, as his dad would say.

As a shadow appeared at the end of the alley, Jimmy James felt his chest tighten.

"Jimmy James?" Fear rippled through the soft tone.

He sucked in a breath as he realized who it was.

Kenzie.

He'd asked her to stay where she was. But, clearly, she hadn't done that.

Unease crept through his muscles.

Through gritted teeth, he said, "Stay back, Kenzie."

Despite his warning, she came closer. Her skin looked pale as she glanced back and forth between Benjamin and Jimmy James.

"Is everything . . . okay?" Her voice trembled.

"That's what I'm trying to figure out."

She gasped as she glanced at the man pinned against the wall. "You're . . ."

"He's one of the guys who gave you a hard time back in Lantern Beach."

"He followed us?"

"No! I didn't. Not on purpose. You've got to believe me."

Jimmy James narrowed his gaze. Showing any

sign of weakness would only make this guy think he was getting off the hook. "I'm going to need to talk to your boss and verify what you just told me."

"Look, man. Call him. He'll verify what I told you is true. I promise."

Still holding on with one hand, Jimmy James pulled the phone from his pocket with the other. "Give me his number."

Benjamin rattled off the numbers, and Jimmy James dialed as he did so. He put the device on speaker so the conversation would be clear to everyone here.

A moment later, a rumbling voice with a deep Southern accent came across the line.

"Is this Julius?" Jimmy James started.

"It is. Who is this?" The man got right to the point.

"This is . . . Captain Jimmy James Gamble. I'm here with someone who claims to be your first mate."

"You talking about Little Benny?"

Jimmy James stared at the scrappy man pressed against the wall. "Yes, Benjamin."

"Yeah, he's my first mate. Did he get himself into trouble or something?"

Jimmy James contemplated his words, giving another hard stare to Little Benny. "I'm just trying to verify which ports you guys have stayed at over the past week."

Julius let out a grunt. "Started in Wilmington. Went to Virginia Beach. Now Cape Charles. Why?"

"Because this guy keeps popping up wherever I go, and I'm starting to get suspicious."

"Sounds like you picked a popular navigation path. I don't know what to tell you."

Jimmy James finally released the man's shirt and stepped back. "That's all I need to know. Thank you."

As he put his phone away, Little Benny stared at him, a gleam of satisfaction in his gaze. "Do you have enough information now?"

Jimmy James let his glare speak loud and clear. "I do. But I don't want to see you around us again. Do you understand?"

Little Benny raised his hands in the air and scooted away. "I understand. I'm not trying to cause trouble. I'll be out of your hair . . . now and in the future."

Jimmy James hoped the man was telling the truth . . . otherwise, they were going to have to go through this again.

But he wouldn't be as nice next time.

———

AS LITTLE BENNY SCURRIED AWAY, Kenzie stared at Jimmy James.

She'd always known the man was tough and strong. But perhaps she hadn't realized that he was so . . . powerful. A tremble rushed through her.

"Kenzie . . ." As Jimmy James reached for her, she froze.

She'd seen this protective side of him before, so she wasn't sure why it was throwing her off balance now.

Hope faded from his eyes. "I can explain."

She stared at him. He was mostly a shadow in the dark alley. A large, strong shadow.

She remembered the tender look in his eyes earlier, and her heart slowed.

Somehow, she knew he'd never hurt her. But that didn't mean what she'd just witnessed didn't shake her up.

"Let's move to somewhere with more light," she suggested.

Jimmy James put his hand on the small of her back and guided her out of the alley. As streetlights lit the air around them, they found a bench and sat.

Jimmy James turned toward her and studied her face.

Kenzie knew without a doubt that her opinion was important to him. She knew he was waiting to hear what she'd say. But, first, he needed to explain.

He cleared his throat as he looked at her. "That man—Little Benny—has shown up at more than one harbor on this trip. Tonight, I had a feeling he was watching us. Then I saw him running, and that's why I went after him. After everything that's happened, I couldn't take any chances."

She supposed that made sense. "But he didn't admit to being behind anything, did he?"

"No. You heard me call his captain, who verified that Cape Charles was indeed on their itinerary." Jimmy James lowered his voice. "Listen, I'm sorry, Kenzie. I didn't mean to scare you."

She rubbed her arms. "This whole situation has scared me."

"I wouldn't blame you if you wanted to leave the boat and return to your old life. No one would want to stay under these circumstances."

She glanced up at him, surprised by the sincerity in his voice. "But that's not what I want."

He gently touched a strand of her hair and pushed it behind her ear. "I'm not going to let anything happen to you."

His words—both tender and full of promise—caused her cheeks to flush with warmth. She knew that he meant what he'd said. For some reason, he had staked claim as her guardian.

And Kenzie wasn't complaining. She liked knowing that somebody was watching out for her. It was especially nice since she'd felt so alone lately.

She finally offered a smile. "Thank you."

A grin curled at the side of his lips, but it quickly faded. "Of course."

They stared at each other another moment before finally Jimmy James rose and offered his hand to help her up. He let out a sigh before saying, "Maybe we should get back now."

She nodded, unable to deny the disappointment that filled her. Why did she long to spend more time with Jimmy James? It seemed to defy logic.

Sometimes the heart wanted what the heart wanted.

But that didn't mean her heart always got its way.

"That's probably a good idea." But the words sounded forced as they left her lips.

As Kenzie slipped her hand into Jimmy James',

she felt a jolt that made the air leave her lungs. Quickly, she stood and released her grip then rubbed her palm against her side.

So much was happening at once.

And she had to figure out what she was going to do about it . . . before someone else got hurt.

CHAPTER TWENTY-FOUR

JIMMY JAMES HADN'T MEANT to frighten Kenzie. In fact, that was the last thing he wanted to do. But he'd seen her guard go up after his confrontation with Little Benny, and he couldn't blame her for being shaken.

Her earlier words had meant so much to him. The fact that she said she believed in him made him feel like he could walk on water.

She was the daughter of a prominent surgeon, and Jimmy James was the son of a fisherman. He shouldn't even entertain the idea that the two of them might ever have a chance together.

Besides, he was the captain of this boat, and Kenzie was officially one of his crew members. It would be improper and unprofessional if he were to pursue anything romantic with her.

So why couldn't he get the thought out of his head?

They reached the boat, and he helped her aboard before turning toward her. She looked absolutely stunning as the moon highlighted her hair.

Would it be crazy to give up the chance of being captain just for the possibility of being with Kenzie?

That answer was a definite yes.

The chances that someone like Kenzie would choose to be with him were minimal, no matter what his heart said.

He swallowed hard as he tried to accept that reality. "It was fun tonight, Kenzie."

She flashed a grin. "It was fun. Thank you for the coffee and the talk."

Jimmy James shoved his hands into his pockets before he did anything stupid like reaching out and pulling her closer. "It was good to get to know you better. I'm glad we ended up on this boat together, despite the circumstances."

"Me too." She nodded toward the stairs. "I guess I should probably turn in for the night. Who knows what kind of antics Buster and his crew are going to be up to tomorrow? I'll need to be well rested."

Her words made him smile because they were so true. "You're right. But not all guests aboard are going to be such a handful."

"Let's hope not."

He walked her inside and to the stairway leading down to her cabin.

She paused on the top step. "It's awfully quiet, isn't it?"

"The crew must be enjoying the time off—other than Sunni."

Kenzie frowned. "I hope she didn't mind staying aboard too much."

"She probably did, but she'll be okay."

Kenzie glanced up and gave him another smile. "Good night, Jimmy James. I figured I'd use your name one more time before you have to go back to being Captain Gamble."

"Goodnight, Stew Kenzie."

As he watched her disappear downstairs, his heart pounded inside his chest.

He had never met somebody like Kenzie Anderson before.

Something about her made Jimmy James want to be a better man.

He was working on it.

But would all his changes come too late for him to get what he really wanted?

———

KENZIE FELT like she was practically glowing as she headed down the steps to her room. There was something about the way she felt when Jimmy James looked at her. . . it almost felt like she was walking on clouds.

She couldn't say she'd ever felt this way before. If circumstances were different, she would have wanted nothing more than to stay upstairs and keep talking to him. Keep spending time with him.

Although there had been a hiccup tonight when he'd chased that man, that didn't really change anything.

Or did it?

She frowned.

Durango had indicated that Jimmy James' jail time was for more than petty crimes—and that it was because he'd hurt somebody. Initially, Kenzie couldn't see Jimmy James ever doing that. Seeing how he'd cornered that man tonight . . . he was definitely capable.

But he also seemed to have self-control. He seemed to have learned from his mistakes.

Did she know what she was getting into? What if Jimmy James *was* dangerous?

No . . . she stood behind her earlier conviction that she didn't think he'd ever hurt her.

Either way, his actions hadn't been out of hate or spite. He'd been trying to track down the person who'd killed Captain Bridgemore. His intentions had been good.

It was just that Kenzie had been thrown into this whole other world, and she was still trying to navigate what her new normal was going to look like.

She reached the door to her bunkroom and pushed it open.

As she did, she saw somebody in her room.

Not just in her room . . . but going through her suitcase.

CHAPTER TWENTY-FIVE

KENZIE LET OUT a breath as she realized what was happening. "Sunni?"

Her bunkmate twirled around, her eyes wide as she stared at Kenzie.

"Kenzie? I wasn't expecting you back yet." She let out a nervous laugh before her gaze hardened with deniability.

Kenzie crossed her arms, knowing she couldn't take it easy on her crewmate. This was unacceptable —whatever her excuse might be. "Why are you going through my things?"

Sunni glanced at the suitcase on the bed before shrugging. There was no way the woman could deny what she was doing. She'd been caught red-handed.

"I thought my tank top might have been mixed up with your laundry," she finally said.

Kenzie doubted that. "So, you went through my things without asking? Twice? What's the real story? Don't tell me another lie."

"Twice? No, I didn't go through your things twice."

"Sunni..."

"That part is the truth!" Sunni let out a sigh, and her eyes shifted back and forth as if she tried to think of an excuse. Finally, her jaw hardened as she stared at Kenzie. "I was just trying to find out some more information about you."

Kenzie let out a breath at the absurdity of her words. "What are you talking about?"

"I mean, you come onto this charter out of the blue. Most of us in the business know each other. Or we know *of* each other, at least. But you just show up out of nowhere and join this crew. That's suspicious."

"Okay . . ." She still wasn't sure what Sunni was getting at.

"Then you're the one who discovers the captain's body? Something just isn't adding up. All of us feel like we could be in danger. So, we're trying to find answers."

Realization spread through Kenzie, and she shook her head. "Wait . . . you think I had something to do with Captain Bridgemore's death?"

Her gaze hardened. "I think someone in the charter boat industry had something to do with it. I know the rest of the guys on the crew. There's no way they would do anything like that. That just leaves you or our new captain."

Kenzie couldn't believe what she was hearing. "Why would I kill Captain Bridgemore?"

"That's what I want to figure out. Who are you really, Kenzie Anderson?" Sunni narrowed her eyes as she stared at Kenzie.

"If you'd bothered to have a conversation with me, you might know. I'm from Delaware. My father is a doctor. I was in med school, but I dropped out because that's not what I want for my future. Instead, I came here to work on the boat and see if this industry is something I'd like to try to make a career of."

Sunni raised an eyebrow. "You went from trying to be a doctor to trying to be a steward?"

Kenzie shrugged, knowing it sounded like a big leap. "Like I said, that's what I'm trying to figure out."

Sunni let out a grunt as if she didn't believe her.

Kenzie wasn't going to play this game. "By the

way, where is Laney? Aren't you supposed to be watching her?"

"For your information, Sylvia came back and got her so they could get ice cream together and look at the stars." The skeptical look remained in her eyes. "You're trying to change the subject, aren't you?"

Kenzie ignored her question. "Whatever you think I may have done it doesn't give you the right to go through my things," she told Sunni. "And, for that matter, I'm not comfortable sharing the same room with you anymore."

Sunni's eyes narrowed as if she were offended. "Fine. I'll take the bottom bunk in Durango's room. At least for the remainder of this trip."

Sunni snatched a few items of clothing from her bunk before storming down the hallway.

She was the one who was upset? Kenzie shook her head in disbelief.

Either way, it didn't matter. This problem paled in comparison to the real issues at hand.

Primarily, the issue of who had killed the captain.

JIMMY JAMES SAT in his chair on the bridge and stared at the dark water in front of him. As he did, his mind raced through everything that had happened, and unease churned in his stomach.

But instead of concentrating on everything that had gone wrong, he turned his thoughts to Kenzie. She was much more pleasant to think about.

Tonight had been surprisingly nice. As hard as Jimmy James tried, he couldn't get the image of Kenzie out of his mind.

She was so beautiful. So pure.

And so out of his league.

He frowned.

Soon, they'd return to the Lantern Beach harbor. Another captain would most likely take his place on *Almost Paradise*. And Kenzie would either continue her commitment to this boat for another seven weeks or she would leave for another opportunity.

The thought of her being out to sea without someone watching her back made Jimmy James' spine tighten. It wasn't that he didn't think she was capable. It was just that he'd seen all the bad things that could happen in life. He'd *experienced* a lot of them. And he didn't want someone as sweet as Kenzie to experience that kind of trauma and heartache.

Still, she was her own person and could choose whatever she wanted to do. Jimmy James was powerless to stop her, and he knew that.

He shifted the metal ball bearings in his hands. Whenever he needed to think, he rotated them between his fingers. A friend had suggested it, and the action always helped to calm him.

As he stared across the water, he realized the boat was still quiet. As far as he knew, he, Kenzie, Sunni, and Laney were the only ones onboard. Buster and his group were still out filming whatever crazy stunts they were trying to get attention for. The rest of the crew was probably out partying.

Jimmy James would enjoy a little bit of quiet. He couldn't go to sleep until everybody was safely onboard again.

As somebody knocked at the door, he turned and saw Chef Durango standing there, his eyes droopy with sleep and his hair disheveled.

"I figured you were out with the rest of the crew." Jimmy James braced himself for more bad news. This trip had apparently programmed him to expect the worst.

"I was, but I came back early to get some rest. As I lay in bed, I thought I heard something." He scratched his head, still looking confused. "Is Siv here?"

"If he's not out with the others, he's probably resting so he can take over at the helm tonight. Why?"

His expression tightened as he shrugged. "I just thought I heard someone in the engine room. When I started down to check, the door leading into it slammed shut. I tried it, but it was locked. It seems weird that someone would be down there at this time."

Jimmy James' spine tightened, and he rose to his feet. "You're right. That is unusual."

If somebody else was on this boat, then he needed to find him. Now.

CHAPTER TWENTY-SIX

KENZIE HEARD footsteps thundering down the hall and froze. Just as she stuck her head out the door, she spotted Jimmy James storming her way.

Alarm rushed through her. Something was clearly wrong.

He paused in front of her, his shoulders and jaw stiff. "Are you in your room alone?"

She nodded, anxious to know what was going on, especially when she heard the urgency in his voice. "Sunni went to Durango's room . . ."

"What about Laney? I thought Sunni was with her."

"Sunni said Laney's mom came and got her."

He locked gazes with her. "I need you to find Sunni, and the two of you need to stay together."

Her heart rate quickened. "What's going on?"

He leaned closer and lowered his voice. "I think somebody uninvited may be aboard the boat."

Kenzie sucked in a deep breath as the implications of his words swept through her mind. Did he mean they had a stowaway?

"What are you going to do?" she asked.

"I'm going to see if I can find him." Jimmy James took a step back. Clearly, there was no time to waste. "Durango and Siv are helping me."

As he stepped away, she started to reach for him. "Jimmy James . . ."

She dropped her hand instead. She had no business touching him. He was her captain.

He paused long enough to look back at her, and he seemed to see the concern in her gaze.

His shoulders softened for just a moment. "I'll be careful. I promise. Okay?"

Kenzie nodded, wishing the worst-case scenarios would stop racing through her head—scenarios that ended up with Jimmy James hurt. With other crew members hurt. With their guests hurt.

Nothing good would come from having a stowaway.

His gaze locked with hers. "Now, I need you to find Sunni and stay with her. Understand?"

Kenzie nodded again, although staying with Sunni was the last thing she wanted to do.

Despite that, she hurried to Durango's room at the end of the hallway and knocked at the door. As she did, she took one last look at Jimmy James as he strode away.

Dear Lord, please help him to be okay. Protect him.

Releasing a pent-up breath, she waited another moment at the door, but the chief stew still didn't answer. Finally, she twisted the handle. "Sunni?"

She pushed the door open, but the space was empty.

Where had Sunni gone? What if the woman was somewhere alone right now and in danger?

Kenzie hurried back to her bunkroom and grabbed her radio. She lifted it to her mouth and said Sunni's name.

But there was no answer.

The chief stew probably didn't have the device on her since it was after hours.

Kenzie's heart thumped in her chest. Should she search for her? Or just lock herself in her room?

She wasn't sure what the right answer was. But if something happened to Sunni, then Kenzie wouldn't be able to live with herself.

She needed to see if she could find her.

With a new resolve in her step, she headed down the hallway looking for her crewmate.

Kenzie searched the crew's quarters, but Sunni was nowhere to be found.

For all she knew, Sunni could have gone out to meet the rest of the crew after all. It was hard to say.

Maybe she should look upstairs.

She hoped that wouldn't be a mistake.

———

JIMMY JAMES QUIETLY—AND carefully—began walking through one of the engine rooms. He didn't want to announce his presence and give a possible intruder the upper hand.

There were lots of spaces a person could hide down here—behind the engine compartments and thrusters and emergency control valves.

Who would have been down here?

Even more important: what was this person doing?

He walked through the first room, peering around each piece of equipment.

Nothing out of the ordinary caught his eye.

Cautiously, he stepped into the second room.

Again, he glanced around, looking for any signs of movement.

Again, nothing.

But tension continued to tighten around his spine.

He stopped at a door tucked away in the corner and pulled on the handle. It wouldn't budge. The sign across the front said, "Owner's Closet." Mr. Robertson must keep his private items here.

Since Jimmy James couldn't get in, he assumed the intruder couldn't either.

As he rounded the corner into the final engine room, a shuffle caught his ear.

Before he could react, something hard hit his head.

Pain spread through his skull.

Then everything went black.

CHAPTER TWENTY-SEVEN

KENZIE LET OUT a breath when she saw Sunni appear around the corner.

She was here, and she was okay.

But where had she been?

Based on the direction she walked from, she could have been in the engine room.

Kenzie's lungs tightened at the thought.

"Sunni." Kenzie put her hands on her hips and didn't bother to hide the relief in her voice. "I've been looking for you."

She scowled as she continued forward, heading toward Kenzie as if annoyed by this interruption. "Is that right? Can't imagine why."

"There may be an intruder on the boat." Kenzie didn't waste time addressing Sunni's snarky comment. "Captain Gamble wants us to stay together while he searches the boat."

Sunni froze and stared at Kenzie, seeming authentically shocked. "Really?"

"Really."

"Why would someone else be on the boat?" Sunni twisted her head as if she thought Kenzie was playing a joke on her or something.

Kenzie didn't understand the woman's resistance, but she didn't want to stand here and argue either. Instead, she nodded toward the bunkrooms. "I don't know. But maybe we should talk about it in my room."

"I think I'd rather stay by myself." Sunni narrowed her eyes as if remembering how much she disliked Kenzie and then turned with a huff to go past her.

As she did, footsteps rushed toward the stairs. The next instant, a man dressed in black from head to toe charged toward them.

Based on his body language, he was about to push Sunni out of the way so he could escape.

"Sunni!" Kenzie grabbed her arm and jerked her away.

The man shoved Kenzie instead. Her back hit the wall before she sank to the floor.

Sunni shrieked as she stared at the intruder.

The man darted away.

Kenzie wanted to run after him. To catch him. To demand answers.

But she couldn't.

Her head was spinning too much for her to move.

JIMMY JAMES SPRINTED down the hall, ignoring the pulsing in his head.

He froze when he saw Sunni kneeling beside Kenzie on the floor.

He rushed to them, concern filling him until he could hardly breathe. "Are you okay?"

Kenzie nodded even though her gaze looked dazed and her motions stiff as she rubbed the back of her head. "I'm okay. Go get him."

Jimmy James took another step but paused, not wanting to leave her. He glanced at Kenzie again, concerned that she could have a concussion.

Kenzie waved her hand at him, her voice raspy as she said, "I'm positive. Go. Really."

With one last hesitant look, he charged upstairs

toward the guest quarters. He glanced around, but didn't see the man anywhere.

Where had that guy gone?

The most logical place would be toward the gangplank.

Jimmy James raced that way. Just as he reached the top deck, he spotted a shadowy figure running on the beach.

He started after him. But before he could get offboard, a car pulled up on the road next to the beach and the man jumped inside.

Jimmy James watched the vehicle race away. The darkness and the distance made it impossible to get a good look at the plates, unfortunately.

He stared after the vehicle and scowled.

What had that guy been doing onboard? Had he been looking for something?

He'd have to figure that out later. Right now, he wanted to check on Kenzie.

The sight of her on the floor—and potentially injured—had caused a knot to form in his chest. That knot of concern quickly turned into a knot of anger.

What had that man done?

He reached the top of the stairway and saw Kenzie standing with her hand at the back of her head with Sunni beside her. He rushed toward Kenzie and paused, probably standing a little too close, but he blamed it on the tight quarters.

"Are you sure you're okay?" he murmured.

Kenzie's face looked pinched and her gaze cloudy.

"I'm fine." Her voice sounded softer than usual, and discomfort showed in her gaze. "That man just shoved me when he went past. It's nothing. Really."

Jimmy James continued to study her, not sure if he believed her response. She seemed like the type who didn't like it when people made a big deal over her. This attention probably wasn't welcome.

But this was no time to put up a façade.

"Did you catch him?" Kenzie's voice lifted with momentary hope as she looked at him.

He frowned as he remembered watching the guy get away. "A car was waiting for him by the shore. He's gone."

Kenzie's shoulders seemed to deflate. "What was he doing in here?"

Jimmy James' jaw stiffened. That was exactly his question.

"That's what we need to find out," he muttered. "Our safety may depend on it."

CHAPTER TWENTY-EIGHT

KENZIE AND SUNNI were assigned to guard the gangplank in case any crew or guests returned before the search was finished. As they did, Durango, Siv, and Jimmy James looked for any evidence as to what the intruder had been doing.

The police had already been called.

As Kenzie stood near the railing, she rubbed her head, which still throbbed.

She knew she'd be okay. She'd simply hit her head, and the Tylenol she took should help her feel better soon. Still, the whole incident had left her shaken.

Right now, she glanced over the water to the harbor beyond.

Was the man who'd been on the boat hiding

somewhere out there now, watching? She knew Jimmy James had said the man jumped into a car. But what if he hadn't gone far?

What exactly was going on here?

Whatever it was, it left her feeling unsettled and wanting off this boat.

It was too bad she had nowhere else to go.

"By the way, I guess I should say thank you."

Sunni's voice pulled Kenzie from her thoughts. She glanced in her crewmate's direction, puzzled by the sudden kindness in her voice.

"Thank you for what?" Kenzie asked.

"You pulled me out of that man's way, and then you ended up getting hurt. That was pretty noble of you." Sunni pressed her lips together as if it pained her to say the words.

Had Sunni just complimented her? Kenzie knew better than to point it out—even if she really wanted to. "It's no problem. I'm sure you would have done the same for me."

As Kenzie said the words, she realized she wasn't sure they were true at all.

"Look, I know we've gotten started on the wrong foot, and that's mostly my fault." Sunni frowned as she heaved in and out a long breath. "I'm sorry. I'm not very trusting of new people."

"I know what that can be like." *Those* words were completely true.

"To be honest, a friend of mine was supposed to be on the crew with me. But she decided to go on a different boat at the last minute, and I've been bummed about it ever since. But it's probably better this way. I usually find it's better if I don't like my stews too much. It makes it easier when I have to put them in their place."

Her words didn't completely make sense. "But you seem to like the rest of the crew okay. You're friends with them."

Sunni shrugged. "The rest of the crew isn't under me. You are. The boating industry can be a man's world, which means I have to try even harder if I want to be on top. It's all a delicate balance."

"I understand." Even though Kenzie might understand, she didn't think that Sunni had the right to treat people poorly just so she could be the boss babe on the ship. This didn't seem like the time to share that feedback, however.

"Who do you think that guy was?" Sunni leaned against the railing, the cracks in her voice making her sound earnestly frightened over what had happened.

Kenzie shrugged. "I have no idea. If a thief

boarded this boat, I'd think he'd go into the guest quarters to look for money or jewelry. But why the engine room?"

Sunni frowned and stared out over the water. "Good point. I don't know. I have to wonder that myself, though."

"Maybe the captain, Siv, and Durango found some answers." Kenzie was getting anxious to hear from them. It felt like they'd been searching the boat for hours. In reality, it had probably been fifteen minutes.

"We can only hope." But Sunni's frown indicated that she didn't feel much more hopeful than Kenzie did.

JIMMY JAMES PULLED out his flashlight so he could better see into the recesses of the engine room.

What had that man been doing down here? It made no sense why someone might be in here unless perhaps he wanted to sabotage the boat. But why? Could it have something to do with the captain's murder? Or was this incident unrelated?

His thoughts sloshed back and forth in his mind.

A footstep sounded in the doorway, and he turned to see Durango standing there.

"I've checked the top deck, but I didn't see anything," Durango said. "And I just got a call for a pickup. I was about to radio Eddie to see if he could handle it."

Jimmy James shone his light behind more of the equipment, but he saw nothing. "You might need to handle this pickup yourself, especially if Eddie has been drinking, which I suspect he has."

Durango frowned but nodded. "I can arrange pickup for them. No problem."

"Perfect." That would give Jimmy James a chance to look at the rest of this area in private.

Because he was determined to get to the bottom of what was going on here.

He waited until he heard Durango climbing the steps.

Then he paced over to a cubbyhole where some tools had been stored.

As he shone his light inside, his spine stiffened.

Was there something down there?

He reached into the space and pulled out a black bag. The sack had blended in with the shadows. If he hadn't had his flashlight, Jimmy James would have never seen it.

He set the package on top of one of the engine compartments, put his flashlight back into his pocket, and then carefully tugged the bag open.

What he saw inside took his breath away.

Six bricks of cocaine were inside . . . and, based on Jimmy James' experience, the stash was probably worth at least one hundred thousand dollars.

CHAPTER TWENTY-NINE

KENZIE COULD HARDLY BREATHE when she walked onto the bridge for another crew meeting.

Jimmy James definitely looked tenser than he had before as he stood silently near the helm. His jaw appeared to flex and unflex. His muscles looked rock solid with tension.

Had something else happened? Did he know something that she didn't?

She took her place against the back wall and waited to find out.

The last half hour had been a whirlwind.

Buster and his crew had returned, and everyone had been asked to look through their things to make sure their belongings were all there. Kenzie halfway expected to hear that some of Sylvia's jewelry was missing. It seemed the most obvious thing that someone might have grabbed. But nothing was gone.

Afterward, their guests had disappeared into their rooms, looking utterly exhausted and slightly frightened.

The crew also looked exhausted. It was four a.m., and most of them would need to be on duty by six.

Finally, after standing silently for what felt like hours, Jimmy James addressed everyone in the room, his gaze hard and probing. "Does anybody know anything about the cocaine I found downstairs in the engine room?"

Kenzie sucked in a breath at his words.

Drugs? Was *that* what this all went back to?

The rest of the crew looked just as stunned as she felt.

No one said anything for a moment until finally Eddie stepped forward. "I don't know anything about it. But I think I can speak for the rest of the crew when I say that none of us are involved with this."

Jimmy James narrowed his eyes. "Somehow, these drugs got on the boat. I need to figure out how they got here, and if any one of you might be somehow connected."

"Did you ever think about talking to Buster?" Eddie's voice sounded cool with accusation. "He seems like the most likely culprit here if you ask me."

Kenzie's heart seemed to still at his allegation. She had a feeling this conversation might turn even uglier than it already was.

"It seems clear that whoever broke onto the boat tonight was looking for something, most likely these drugs." Jimmy James paced in front of the group, the set of his shoulders daring anyone to lie to him. "So, the question is: who was the person? How did he know the drugs were here? Has he been following us our entire itinerary waiting for the opportunity to get his hands on it? More importantly, do these drugs have anything to do with Captain Bridgemore's murder?"

Again, no one said anything.

But Kenzie knew his questions were valid. Something dirty was going on. Even though part of her didn't want to think that someone on this boat could be involved, that conclusion made the most sense.

Jimmy James paused in front of Eddie and looked him square in the eye. "Eddie, you know the owner of this boat, Mr. Robertson. Where was his boat docked before it came to Lantern Beach?"

Eddie shrugged, almost as if annoyed by the question. "Mr. Robertson splits his time between Charlotte and Bermuda. But, from what I understand, he usually likes to dock the boat in Hatteras."

"Then why did he base his charter out of Lantern Beach?" Jimmy James asked.

"He thought people might enjoy the small island charm. Plus, I think it was cheaper. I don't know, to be honest. It's not like I asked him."

Kenzie wondered if it had something to do with regulations. A bigger marina like the one in Hatteras would have more oversight than the smaller one in Lantern Beach.

Jimmy James scanned everyone in the room before he growled out a warning. "If I find out any of you are involved in this, not only will you leave this boat, but I will report you to the police. Do you understand?"

Kenzie's heart pounded harder into her chest. She had no doubt he was serious—as he should be. If a member of the crew brought drugs aboard—or if they were using drugs onboard—then Jimmy James could lose his license.

"Why are you looking at us?" Defensiveness edged Eddie's voice at the captain's words. "Who's to say that *you're* not the one responsible?"

Jimmy James narrowed his eyes as he stepped toward Eddie. "Why would I bring drugs on this boat?"

Eddie stared back defiantly. "Maybe for the same reason you wanted at the last moment to be the captain. Who knows what kind of things you're up to?"

Kenzie saw the anger simmering in Jimmy James' eyes, but he held it back as he stared off with Eddie.

"I didn't bring drugs on this boat." His words sounded hard, and his stance made it clear he wasn't someone to be messed with.

Eddie stepped closer, almost as if he were on a roll and felt invincible. "How can we know that? After all, you may present yourself as someone who's reformed and who likes to follow the rules. But we all know that's not the case, is it?"

Jimmy James squared his shoulders, fumes practically rising from his skin. "What's *that* supposed to mean?"

"I'm pretty sure there's a rule that the captain isn't supposed to fraternize with the crew." Eddie glanced at Kenzie and smirked. "They're *definitely* not supposed to date the crew."

Kenzie held back a gasp. What was Eddie insinuating?

"I'm not dating anyone on the crew," Jimmy James stated, his voice as hard as his jaw.

"Oh yeah?" Eddie wiggled his head in a cocky manner. "That's not what I saw tonight."

The captain's hands went to his hips and his chest seemed to broaden as he bristled. "What are you talking about?"

"I saw the two of you in the alley," Eddie continued, a smug look in his eyes as his gaze flickered from Kenzie to Jimmy James. "It looked like the two of you were more than just friendly to me."

Kenzie wasn't going to stand back while he threw out these accusations. "Captain Gamble and I didn't cross any lines. I don't know what you *thought* you saw, but all the two of us did was talk."

Eddie grunted as if he didn't believe her. Then he shrugged again and turned back to the captain. "All I'm saying is that maybe our captain is pointing fingers at us so nobody will look at him."

Kenzie felt the situation growing out of control and felt tension thread through her. The crew would be no good to each other if distrust formed walls between them. She had to put an end to this.

"Maybe we all just need to get some sleep,"

Kenzie said. "Our emotions are riled up right now. We're tired. No one is thinking straight."

"Of course, you would say that," Eddie muttered. "You just want to defend your little boyfriend."

"Lay off her." Sunni's voice contained an edge of defensiveness. "Kenzie is right. I think we should all get some sleep and then meet again later."

"Agreed," Jimmy James said. "Buster requested brunch, so we'll be able to start our day a little later than usual. I suggest you all go and try to get some sleep. Lock your doors tonight, just to be safe. Owen, you have duty tonight, right?"

"Yes, Captain." Owen nodded.

"Stay vigilant," Jimmy James said. "The rest of you, get some sleep."

Dread formed in Kenzie's stomach at his words. But Jimmy James was right. They needed to be careful until they knew who was behind this and what was going on.

Tonight's intruder may have run off the boat.

But that didn't mean that somebody onboard wasn't helping him.

JIMMY JAMES SUSPECTED he wouldn't get any sleep in the few hours left of the night.

But he *definitely* wouldn't get any sleep until he had a heart-to-heart conversation with Eddie. The first mate had been out of line earlier, and he didn't appreciate the insubordination.

"Eddie," he called before the man left the room. "I need a few minutes of your time."

As he said the words, Eddie's entire demeanor changed from defiant to fearful. He hadn't expected to be called out, had he?

Good. The man needed to be put in his place.

When everyone else was gone, Jimmy James closed the door behind him before standing in front of it with his arms crossed. The position was meant to intimidate. Eddie might be cocky and defiant, but he was almost spineless.

"I don't appreciate you calling me out in front of the rest of the crew like that," Jimmy James started.

Eddie's eyes wavered a moment before he raised his gaze to meet Jimmy James'. "I think it's only fair to let people know you could be the culprit. I looked into you. I know you've been in some trouble."

"Maybe I have been in the past. But that's not who I am today."

"Honestly, I don't think that people really

change." He raised a shoulder in an off-handed shrug.

Something about his words hit Jimmy James like a punch in the face. "Is that right? You don't even think that you've changed?"

"I always try, but somewhere deep inside me, I'm still the person I've always been. I always go back. All it takes is one moment of losing self-control."

"And what does that look like for you?" Jimmy James narrowed his eyes, curious about his statement. "What happens when you lose that self-control? Is it an anger issue? Narcissism? Or maybe it's even drugs."

Eddie raised his chin as if he hadn't expected the conversation to go in this direction. "You don't know what you're talking about."

"I'm just asking you to clarify your statement."

Eddie stared another moment, his jaw shifting as if he were grinding his teeth. Finally, he shrugged stiffly. "My vices are simpler than that. Basically, I'll do anything for a pretty woman. But not drugs, if that's what you're thinking."

"You're full of contradictions, aren't you?" Jimmy James had this guy's number.

Eddie was a fast talker. Quick to jump to conclusions. Easy to charm and lead. But it was all surface with no depth to anchor him.

Jimmy James' talk with him had thrown Eddie off course.

"I'm just trying to get to the bottom of what's going on, just like you," Eddie insisted.

Jimmy James stepped closer, determined to drive home his point. "Let me make myself clear. If you speak to me in front of the crew like that one more time, you're off this boat. Without pay. I will *not* tolerate disrespect. Whether you like me or not isn't the point. The fact of the matter is that I am your captain. Do you understand?"

Defiance still remained in Eddie's eyes, but it lessened as he nodded. "Understood."

"Now, get out of here."

After Eddie left, Jimmy James sat back in his chair to think.

A clearer picture of what was going on began to form in his head.

Somebody had been paying off Captain Bridgemore for his silence. That silence most likely had something to do with the drugs Jimmy James found.

Maybe the captain had known those bricks of cocaine were there, and he'd chosen to look the other way in return for a cut of the profits.

Jimmy James was surprised the police hadn't found the drugs when they'd boarded the boat in Lantern Beach.

Maybe they hadn't been there then.

Or they may not have found the cocaine because it was so well hidden. Currently, he'd been told to stash the cocaine in a safe in his quarters until he could turn it in to the authorities.

But his questions still lingered.

Who had the captain been working with? Could it be a member of the crew?

That wasn't out of the question.

The person on the boat tonight could have simply been a runner—someone who'd been charged with picking up the drugs and taking them to the dealer. Jimmy James didn't know why, if it was someone on the crew, they wouldn't have just grabbed the stash themselves and taken it some-where. He'd have to think about that a little bit more.

But, right now, he needed to make some deci-sions. As captain, he was in charge of this crew and this trip. He'd been tasked with making the tough calls.

He needed to figure out if he should simply end this charter now and risk losing not only any future job possibilities but also any paycheck. Or should he take his chances and see if they could make it through the next couple of days?

The decision pressed on him, because he knew that the safety of his passengers and crew rested on his shoulders.

CHAPTER THIRTY

KENZIE COULDN'T HELP but notice that every-body seemed more somber the next morning. She couldn't blame anyone for the change. She felt more somber also.

Even Buster and his guests seemed subdued. That could, in part, be a hangover from their wild night of partying. Or maybe the truth was beginning to settle on them—the truth that Waldo was still missing and that this charter hadn't ended up being everything they'd thought it would.

Out of curiosity, Kenzie had checked Buster's YouTube channel this morning. Sure enough, he'd posted a new video of himself demonstrating what it would be like to be hooked like a fish. As she watched in horror, he pressed the end of a fishing hook into his mouth/cheek area and made a big production of acting out the experience.

Why would someone do something like that?

He definitely had a flare for drama.

She only hoped he'd been using a prop, and not a real fishing hook. She didn't know for certain. She'd had to look away.

Right now, she set the table for brunch on the deck. At least the weather looked beautiful even if everyone's moods were gloomy.

If they stayed on schedule, the boat would leave after brunch and head to Baltimore before returning to Lantern Beach. She wasn't sure what would happen after that.

Would a new captain replace Jimmy James? Would the rest of their charters be canceled?

But the even bigger question was, would Captain Bridgemore's killer be identified and arrested? She'd feel better after that happened. Knowing there was a killer at large was disconcerting, to say the least.

As she finished setting the table, she glanced into the parking area and saw a police car pull up. Her heart rate quickened.

Did they have an update on Waldo? On the drugs? Maybe they'd made an arrest.

The rest of the crew must have noticed the police's arrival also. They all seemed to gravitate toward the gangplank in anticipation.

Kenzie stepped onto the deck just in time to hear an officer say, "We found Waldo Alves, and he's not looking good."

JIMMY JAMES BRACED himself for whatever the officer who'd boarded *Almost Paradise* was about to say. But he knew by the man's expression and his words that it wasn't good news.

"What do you mean, he's not looking good?" Jimmy James asked.

The officer—Officer Stabler, as he'd introduced himself—scanned everyone around him. Was he searching people's expressions for any signs of guilt? Looking for deceit?

Most likely.

He turned back to Jimmy James and finally said, "Mr. Alves was found beaten near the boardwalk in Virginia Beach."

Gasps spread through the group.

"I'm sorry to hear that," Jimmy James said. "Not to sound callous, but you came all the way to Cape

Charles to tell us this?"

Officer Stabler held up his badge. "I'm with the Cape Charles PD. Virginia Beach Police called and asked for our assistance on this matter. I'm hoping I can speak with Buster Moreno."

"I'll go get him." Eddie took a step back.

"Actually, I'd like for Durango to go get him," Jimmy James said.

Eddie glared at him, but Jimmy James didn't care. He still didn't trust Eddie, and he wasn't going to let Eddie think that he was in control.

With a nod, Durango left to find Buster. Jimmy James turned back to Officer Stabler, anxious to hear more details. "Is there anything else that you can tell us?"

Officer Stabler's jaw twitched, but his aviator sunglasses concealed his eyes—and anything his expression might give away. "Mr. Alves is currently in stable condition, but he's seriously injured. It's a miracle that the man is even alive."

Before Jimmy James could ask any more questions, Durango appeared with Buster beside him. Buster, with his disgruntled look, didn't appear to appreciate being called away from whatever he was doing. His eyes were red-rimmed and narrow.

"What's going on?" Buster ran a hand through

his hair as he stared at the officer, clearly trying to compose himself. The man was nervous.

Officer Stabler gave him the update on Waldo, and, as he did, Jimmy James watched Buster's expression. Was he behind any of this?

The YouTube star didn't show the initial shock and repulsion that Jimmy James had expected. In fact, his whole reaction seemed lackluster—especially considering Waldo was his best friend.

"He was beaten?" Buster repeated. "What . . . ? How . . . ?"

"I'm hoping you might be able to tell us," Officer Stabler said. "There was a note in Mr. Alves' pocket indicating you may have paid someone to put him in his place."

Jimmy James sucked in a quick breath. Was Buster really that despicable?

"That's ludicrous." Buster's voice rose with defensiveness. "I would never do something like that to my friend. Someone must have set me up."

"Why would someone do that?" Stabler asked, pulling his sunglasses on top of his head and staring at Buster.

Buster shrugged, the action fraught with nervous energy and defensiveness. "I don't know. Maybe they're threatened by my wealth."

"Have you received any threats?" Stabler continued.

"I get weird threats all the time, from parents saying I'm a bad influence on their kids, from women who are mad because I don't want to date them, from sponsors who are irked because I turned down offers. It's part of the business." With every word, Buster's voice rose in pitch.

He was close to panic, wasn't he?

Stabler's jaw jumped but his face otherwise remained stoic. "I'm going to need to see those."

"Of course," Buster rushed. "Whatever you need. Whatever it takes to prove I didn't do this. I didn't hurt my best friend. I do a lot of stupid things, but I'd never go that far. Can I see this note that I *supposedly* wrote?"

"I'm afraid not, but we *are* going to need to get a handwriting sample."

"For a friend, you've certainly done a lot of trash-talking about him ever since he disappeared," Jimmy James muttered, his words pointed.

Buster stepped back and scowled. "I don't know what you're talking about. Sure, Waldo and I had a disagreement. But I fully expected the two of us to be cool again soon. We just needed more time."

"That's one theory." Officer Stabler shrugged as if

skeptical. "But the two of us are going to need to sit down and talk one-on-one."

CHAPTER THIRTY-ONE

KENZIE WISHED she could be a fly on the wall. She wanted to know what Officer Stabler was talking to Buster about. Wanted to know what Buster was saying.

Instead, at Jimmy James' instruction, she got back to work, along with the rest of the crew.

But all she could think was, *Poor Waldo.*

She prayed he'd pull through. She obviously didn't know the man well. But, out of everyone in the group, he'd seemed one of the nicest.

As she continued to straighten the main salon, she kept glancing over at Buster's family and friends. They all seemed to be in shock as they quietly murmured to each other and shook their heads.

But *were* they in shock? If Buster wasn't behind

what happened, could one of them be? After all, Buster was their payday. If money stopped rolling into *his* bank account, then it would also stop rolling into *their* bank accounts.

Was that the realization they all mulled over? Or were they mourning what had happened to Waldo?

Finally, a few minutes later, the officer and Buster emerged from the meeting room where they'd been chatting. Buster's cheeks were red, and he almost reminded her of a child that had been scolded by a parent. He was definitely giving off a bad vibe, one filled with entitlement and attitude.

Officer Stabler offered everyone a nod as he headed back out to the deck. As he did, Jimmy James approached him. The two exchanged a few words before Officer Stabler followed him down the hall.

If Kenzie had to guess, he was retrieving the cocaine that had been found.

Right on cue, they reappeared and Officer Stabler had something in a black bag. A few minutes later, he departed.

Alone.

He hadn't taken Buster with him. Was there not enough evidence to arrest him? Was he still a suspect?

Kenzie didn't know. But curiosity burned inside her.

Buster didn't seem to want the scrutiny, so he returned to his room without another word.

Jimmy James stepped back into the salon to address everyone. "Everything is going to continue as normal. Brunch will be served in twenty minutes. Then we'll be on our way. But instead of heading to Baltimore, we're returning to Lantern Beach."

Murmurs went around the room.

"My apologies that we have to cut this trip short, but given everything that has happened, I don't have much choice," Jimmy James finished.

Kenzie thought he'd made the right decision. But she also knew the choice couldn't have been easy. Certainly, people would be upset with whatever he decided.

Instead of glancing the captain's way and trying to read how he was feeling now, Kenzie continued sweeping crumbs from the floor so they could keep this place spic-and-span.

But she knew that it was going to be much harder to stop thinking about this new turn of events. Another person had been hurt.

How many more would there be before this trip was over?

JIMMY JAMES STOOD at the helm and gripped his phone as he waited for Mr. Robertson to answer. A churn of nerves shuffled in his stomach, but he pushed it down.

Doing the right thing wasn't always easy. No one ever said it would be.

But there was no way he could avoid this conversation.

The man picked up on the second ring, his voice distant and aloof.

Jimmy James had glanced at the weather on his app, double-checking that conditions were safe for their journey, before putting the phone to his ear. "Good morning, sir. This is Captain Jimmy James Gamble."

"What can I do for you, Captain Gamble?" His voice contained an edge of irritation, probably at being interrupted.

Jimmy James hesitated a moment before diving into the update. He wasn't sure how the man would react, but he anticipated it wouldn't be good.

"You've got to be kidding me." Mr. Robertson's voice rose. "How is all this even happening?"

Jimmy James frowned as he stared at the control

panel in front of him, his mind going a million different directions. "That's what the police are trying to figure out, but I have no choice but to cut this charter cruise short."

"You don't have the authority to do that." Each word sounded snipped and tight.

"I have no choice," Jimmy James reiterated. "One of our guests is in the hospital. Cocaine was found in the engine room. The original captain of this boat was murdered. I can't risk anything else happening to my crew or the guests."

Mr. Robertson didn't say anything for a moment before finally growling, "This wasn't your call to make."

"It's my job to make sure everyone is safe, so I'd say that it is."

"If you go against my orders, you're never going to get another job around here. You know that, don't you?" The threat in his voice was clear.

Jimmy James kept his voice professional as he said, "Yes, sir."

"Come back to Lantern Beach if that's what you feel like you have to do. But then the two of us are finished. Do you understand that?"

Jimmy James flexed his jaw as he stared out over the bay. "I got the message loud and clear."

Robertson ended the call without a goodbye.

The conversation wasn't surprising. But, on the other hand, it wasn't what Jimmy James wanted to hear either.

He was just trying to do the right thing. For so long, he hadn't cared about what the right thing might be. Everything had always been about him. About the next high. About how to take the easy path instead of the hard one.

At times, that lifestyle was still tempting. It was a simpler way of thinking. He wouldn't say that it had less consequences, but he could see why someone might think that.

He sat in his captain's chair and leaned back. He thought about Eddie's words from last night—about how people couldn't really change.

He wasn't sure why he was letting that guy get into his head. Yet Jimmy James couldn't help but ponder his first mate's words.

Could people change? Jimmy James wanted to think he was a new man. A *better* man. That was all he'd been focused on the past few years.

Sure, he still had friends from the old days. But he kept them at arm's length.

The old saying that people were known by the company they kept was true, and for that reason

Jimmy James didn't get too close. But he still wanted to be there to support his old friends and to show them that turning their lives around was possible. So that was what he tried to do.

In the process, he'd even been able to get information for the police on occasion, information that helped them solve crimes. It was part of the reason he and Chief Chambers had a good rapport now.

He also knew that heading back to Lantern Beach could permanently kill his dreams. He'd been saving to buy his own boat. To do his own charters. Those things were part of his plan to turn his future around.

Now he'd gone out on a limb trying to help Kenzie, and all that might be ruined.

But when he thought about Kenzie, he didn't feel any regret. All he felt was self-imposed tension as he wondered what it would take to truly keep her safe.

CHAPTER THIRTY-TWO

AS *ALMOST PARADISE* headed away from Cape Charles into the mouth of the Chesapeake Bay and the Atlantic Ocean beyond, Kenzie kept busy by doing laundry. What she really wanted was to talk to Jimmy James alone. However, any time she spent alone with him might paint him in a negative light, and she didn't want to do that.

A bad feeling simmered inside her as she switched a load from the washer to the dryer. Things were going to get worse before they got better, weren't they?

Who could be behind these incidents that had happened? Was someone on the boat involved? If so, who?

She reviewed everyone onboard.

Buster probably had the strongest motive, and his arrogance was definitely a weakness. But he was the type who liked attention for doing stupid things. Going to jail would end his career and stop his cash flow. Kenzie couldn't see him risking that.

Or was he so arrogant that he thought he could get away with it?

Gilbert was constantly looking at his phone and sneaking away. She'd even seen him whispering to Nikki a few times. What was he hiding? There was definitely more to his story.

Then there was Nikki. Buster was known to have an eye for pretty women. Did that make Nikki jealous? Was she trying to sabotage him by harming his best friend? The motive seemed shaky, but people had done crazier things for lesser reasons.

Or what if it wasn't the guests who might be involved with these crimes? What if it was a member of the crew?

Eddie certainly seemed to have a chip on his shoulder, as did Sunni. She still wasn't sure exactly what their stories were, though. Both seemed guarded.

Kenzie couldn't see Owen being guilty, nor could she see Durango or Siv. Maybe the people who flew under the radar were the ones who should be scrutinized the most, though . . .

Kenzie didn't know. But until she had more answers, she couldn't be too trusting of anyone . . . except maybe Jimmy James.

After her loads were switched, she straightened her back and stepped from the laundry room. She needed a breather, and she'd finished her work here for now.

She stepped outside, leaned against the railing of the boat, and stared out at the water a minute, letting the fresh breeze flow over her face and arms.

Right now, they were surrounded by nothing but ocean.

Usually, the sight of water comforted her. But at this moment, that realization caused fear to shoot through her as she realized how isolated they truly were.

JIMMY JAMES STEPPED into the main salon just in time to hear Gilbert wrapping up a conversation on the phone. He stood in the corner with his back toward the empty room—but his voice still carried.

"You don't have to tell me twice. I know the

money will be great, and I can't wait to get my hands on it," he muttered. "Not long now."

Jimmy James felt his back muscles tighten. What was the man talking about?

He had one guess: the cocaine.

Jimmy James cleared his throat. When he did, Gilbert quickly shifted toward him, a startled look on his face.

Jimmy James crossed his arms and stared at the man, making it clear he wasn't going anywhere without an explanation.

Gilbert seemed to realize he'd been caught and shook his head. He pressed a button on his cell phone before sliding it back into his pocket. "That's not what it sounds like."

Jimmy James stepped closer. "What exactly is going on, Gilbert? I'm not the only one who's noticed your strange behavior. And given everything that's happened . . ."

Gilbert raised his hands, sweat invading his skin. "I can explain."

Jimmy James remained stoic. "I'm waiting."

"Nikki and I are doing a real estate deal together," he rushed. "That's the big secret I'm keeping."

Jimmy James narrowed his eyes at the unexpected words. "What?"

"You know she's a realtor. She found a great deal on some property and asked me to go in with her. I'm tired of living off someone else's money—Buster's, mainly—so I decided to try my hand at some investment property."

"Where did you get the money for this real estate deal?" Jimmy James remained cautious, not eager to believe this man without more proof.

"Buster bought his mom a beamer," he rushed. "We sold it and got some money. Quite a bit, actually."

"Does Buster know this yet?"

Gilbert frowned. "No. We're waiting until it goes through before we tell him. We're not sure how he's going to react. He can be a little erratic at times."

That explained the secret conversations he'd seen, Jimmy James supposed.

Before he could ask more questions, the boat almost sounded like it let out a groan.

What was that?

"Excuse me a minute," he muttered before darting back to the bridge. He rushed into the room, where Siv stood at the helm.

"What's going on?" Jimmy James rushed, his gaze scanning the control panel.

"All the dials look okay, but something is clearly wrong. I'll go check the engine room."

Siv rushed away.

As he did, Jimmy James continued to check the panel for any sign of what was wrong.

Considering earlier events, he'd be foolish not to be concerned—on more than one level.

What if the intruder had done something to the engine while he was onboard? If someone was desperate to sneak on board, then they were desperate enough to tamper with the yacht.

A few minutes later, Siv's voice sounded on the radio. "Captain, Captain. It looks like a cylinder has broken. I'm trying to fix it, but . . ."

Concern rushed through Jimmy James. "How did that happen?"

"Looking at the marks on the metal, the only way it happened is if somebody tampered with it."

"Do you think you'll be able to fix it?"

"It's going to take some time and some supplies."

Just as Siv said the words, another grinding sound filled the air, and the boat slowed.

Jimmy James' stomach churned at the sound of it.

The fact that it was purposeful only made the situation worse.

"What do you want me to do, Captain?" Siv asked over the radio.

"See what you can do to fix this. If it looks like that's not possible, I need to know ASAP."

"Will do."

Jimmy James slowed the boat more, knowing that this hiccup would add some time to their trip. But he couldn't continue as if this equipment malfunction wasn't a real issue. He'd need to make an announcement to the crew and guests.

Before he did that, he made a call to Chief Chambers. She needed to know what was going on here. At least one person did.

His next call would be to the Coast Guard.

CHAPTER THIRTY-THREE

"ATTENTION, guests and crew, we're experiencing some engine difficulties," Captain Gamble's voice rang through the intercom system. "We'll be stopping momentarily to address these issues before continuing on our way. At this time, there's nothing to be alarmed about. Please carry on until we have another update for you."

If there was nothing to be alarmed about, why did fear race through Kenzie? There was more to that announcement. She was sure of it.

She lifted the iron from the plaid shirt so she wouldn't get distracted. She'd gone back to work on the laundry, knowing she'd regret it if she got behind.

"What do you think's going on?" Sunni suddenly appeared in the doorway.

"I wish I knew." Kenzie shrugged as she continued to iron Buster's shirt, forcing herself to focus.

"I'm getting nervous. Really nervous." Sunni touched her throat as if it were dry and she was having trouble swallowing.

Kenzie was nervous also, but she didn't say that out loud. She feared it would only make Sunni's panic snowball.

"Just remain vigilant," Kenzie finally said.

Sunni nodded and took a step away. "Buster and his gang are playing poker in the main salon. I've got to go serve them more food and drinks before they get too rowdy."

"Good luck."

Kenzie tried to keep herself busy with ironing, but she couldn't stop thinking about who might be behind everything that had happened on the boat.

Durango's knife had been used as a murder weapon.

Buster seemed to love attention, money, and power. Did he arrange all this thinking it would be an easy way to make some cash?

Or what about Gilbert? What kind of secrets was he harboring?

Kenzie didn't have any of those answers.

Instead, she finished ironing the shirt and grabbed some towels along with the ironed clothes and headed upstairs. As she did, she passed by a window and stared at the ocean surrounding them.

She thought about Jimmy James' announcement.

Something was wrong and she had the feeling *Almost Paradise* hadn't seen the last of its troubles.

"I CAN'T GET THIS FIXED." Siv used a wrench on the engine, trying to repair the pipe.

Jimmy James stared at the engine and frowned. Something had clearly been sabotaged. He'd checked the engine last night, and he hadn't seen any damage. Certainly, he would have noticed something like this.

Had someone come down during the night and done this? He didn't like to think about that possibility, but he'd be a fool not to.

His spine stiffened as he realized what he needed to do.

Jimmy James headed back to the bridge to call for backup.

Clearly, someone had wanted them to be stranded. But why? And where? At the harbor back in Cape Charles? Or out here in the middle of the ocean?

If the answer was out in the middle of the ocean, then somebody wanted to isolate them to cause trouble. Serious trouble.

Deadly trouble.

Jimmy James picked up his radio and glanced out the window.

As he did, he saw a small boat trolling closer.

His heart thumped in his ears. There was only one reason a boat would approach them like this.

Serious trouble had found them.

CHAPTER THIRTY-FOUR

AS KENZIE DELIVERED FRESHLY PRESSED clothes and clean towels to Buster's room, she paused near the window. A small skiff with three men onboard pulled up. Why was the vessel coming so close to the yacht?

She gasped as she realized the truth.

This wasn't happenstance.

That boat was here for a purpose—most likely something involving that cocaine they'd found.

"What is it?" Sunni appeared in the doorway and followed Kenzie's gaze. As she did, she sucked in a quick breath. "Is that . . . ?"

"It's trouble." Alarm raced through Kenzie as she turned toward Sunni. "We need to get all our guests into their rooms and tell them to lock their doors. Pronto."

Sunni's eyes widened. "What's going on?"

Kenzie dropped the clothes and towels on the bed and hurried to the stairs. She knew it was too late to stop these guys from boarding. By the time she got to the deck, they would have time to storm the boat.

Instead, she grabbed the radio from her waist. "All crew, all crew. We've got trouble."

"Trouble?" Eddie said. "What are you talking about?"

"We need to get our guests to safe quarters," Kenzie rushed. "We don't have any time to waste."

The safety of the guests had to be their first priority. This was what the crew had been trained to do—although everyone had hoped they'd never have to use these safety protocols.

"Kenzie, Kenzie," Durango said. "Have you lost your mind?"

"All crew, all crew. Kenzie is right. Men have boarded the boat." Jimmy James' tense voice came through the line, each word sounding slow and purposeful. "I'm with them right now, and they have guns. They're directing me what to say right now.

Everyone needs to remain calm and stay where they are."

Kenzie's heart beat so hard it was almost all she could hear.

These guys were on the boat.

With guns pointed at Jimmy James.

Dread filled her stomach.

No, it was bigger than dread. It was total fear.

Were these guys going to kill them?

WHEN JIMMY JAMES had arrived at the deck, men dressed in all black with guns in their hands had already boarded. The four of them stood on the deck now, Jimmy James with his hands in the air, as he complied with their demands.

He hadn't been able to stop them from boarding.

And now danger zinged through the air as the men stared at him, daring him to make a move.

A step sounded behind him, and Jimmy James turned to see Eddie. The bosun stopped in his tracks when he spotted the gunmen.

His eyes widened. "You weren't joking."

This was the problem with insubordination. If only *this* was the time to make a point.

"Both of you," the leader said. "Inside. Now. If anyone tries anything smart, you're all dead. Do you understand?"

"Nobody needs to get hurt here." Jimmy James stared at the semi-automatic guns, and he knew good and well what kind of damage they could do. "Just tell us what you want."

"What I want right now is for you all to get inside," the leader barked. "Everyone. How many people are on this boat?"

"Twelve."

"Everyone needs to get into the meeting room. And I mean *everyone*. Try to throw any fastballs, and there will be consequences."

Jimmy James had no doubt those words were true.

CHAPTER THIRTY-FIVE

KENZIE FELT her heart stuttering in her chest as she stared at the guns pointed at the crew. The men directed them into the main salon and then through the door there into the meeting room.

The space had no windows, a table at the center, and felt suffocating.

Sunni sniffled before a sob escaped from her. Eddie seemed to try to comfort her. Durango, Siv, and Owen all looked stunned.

Then there was Jimmy James. Every time Kenzie glanced at him, she knew he was trying to calculate a way to stop this. But the men had their guns aimed primarily at him, as if he was the biggest threat.

Maybe he was.

Kenzie still couldn't believe this was happening.

Yet it was all too real.

Dear God . . . please, help us!

Two of the men rounded up all the guests on the boat. Buster and Nikki were the final two shoved into the small meeting room.

Instead of offering any sarcastic remarks, even Buster remained quiet.

Jimmy James stepped toward the men, his body shielding the rest of the people inside the room. "What do you want from us?"

"Things got off schedule," the leader said. "Now, we need to get back on track. Unfortunately, that means there may be collateral damage."

Kenzie's heart continued to thump in her chest as she anticipated what these guys might say or do next.

Nikki was hyperventilating behind her. Gilbert fanned himself. Sunni let out a little cry.

Kenzie didn't want to let herself be weak—not even for a minute. If she did, she might completely crumble. But it was taking a lot of energy to maintain a cool head.

"Collect all their cell phones and radios before we lock them inside this room," the leader said.

"You heard him! Everyone, move!" The second in command raised his gun. "Give me your cell phones and radios. Don't even think about trying to use them."

"Why don't you let us talk this out?" Jimmy James said.

"There will be no talking," the leader said. "Now, move!"

"No one needs to get hurt—"

At his words, the leader grabbed Kenzie's arm and shoved the gun to her temple. "Hand over your radios and cell phones, or I'll shoot her. Don't test me."

All the air left Kenzie's lungs as she realized what was happening. Her head wobbled like she might pass out. No . . .

Jimmy James stared at her, and his eyes widened.

With the shake of his head, he raised his hands. "Okay, okay. We'll do whatever you say. Just don't hurt Kenzie."

***

JIMMY JAMES COULDN'T TAKE his eyes off the scene in front of him.

This guy had Kenzie.

With a gun to her head.

One slip of his finger, and she'd be gone.

He couldn't stomach the thought of it.

That meant Jimmy James couldn't do anything risky, anything that might put her in more danger.

"Stay back!" the leader snarled again as he scooted back with Kenzie in tow. "Don't test me. I mean it!"

"We hear you." Jimmy James raised his hands as he stood in the meeting room, the crew and guests gathered behind him. Everyone handed over their devices—their lifelines in this situation. But they had no choice but to comply. "Just don't hurt anyone."

"We'll see if everyone behaves," the leader said. "No one try anything stupid, and you'll increase your chances of surviving this."

Someone sobbed behind him and was quickly shushed.

The leader's gaze met someone behind Jimmy James, and he nodded in communication. "Siv, let's go."

The next instant, Siv stepped through the group and joined the gunmen as if they were best friends.

"Siv?" Jimmy James muttered, disbelief filling him. It took a lot for someone to pull something over on him, but Siv had succeeded. "What?"

Siv shrugged, his eyes appearing lifeless as he stared at the group.

Jimmy James shook his head, fighting both anger and disappointment. "You're a part of this? You were the mole?"

Siv shrugged again. "Sorry. But my side gig pays better. What can I say?"

The next instant, the door to the meeting room slammed shut, and Jimmy James heard something move in front of it.

His jaw tightened as he turned back to the rest of the group.

They all looked to him for guidance.

He prayed he would make the right choices.

If not, someone—or all of them—might get hurt.

The burden almost felt too big to bear.

CHAPTER THIRTY-SIX

KENZIE TRIED NOT to cry out as the man gripped her arm. He pulled her up the stairs toward the bridge.

Her heart raced with every step. Nothing good was going to come of this. She was certain of it.

She was keenly aware of the gun in the man's hand. The barrel was no longer pressed to her temple, but the man still pointed it at her, ready to use it if necessary.

Something about the man left no doubt he'd pull the trigger—he didn't even need a good reason.

Maybe it was his voice and the way he spoke, like he didn't have a care in the world. Maybe it was his quick motions that didn't show much thought. Or maybe it was the greed in his gaze.

Kenzie wasn't sure. But whatever those traits were, they terrified her.

As he shoved her onto the bridge, he released her arm and she skulked away from him, trying to put as much distance between him and herself as she could.

The leader stripped his mask off, revealing a shock of dark hair, blue eyes, and a beard. He didn't look nearly as scary as she'd thought he would. In fact, it was unnerving how normal he appeared.

"Allow me to introduce myself," he said. "I'm Hank."

Her throat tightened. If this guy was allowing her to see his face, that must mean she wasn't going to walk away from this. It was the only explanation that made sense.

His henchmen gathered around him as he turned to address them.

"So, we grab what we came for, we get back on our boat, then we get out of here," Hank said. "Tom, you still know where that sandbar is?"

"Only about a mile from here. I'll text you the coordinates."

"Perfect. We'll smash their radios, then we run the ship aground. That should buy us some time."

Siv took a step back. "I'll get the rest of the goods."

The goods? Cocaine, Kenzie realized. There must be more hidden on the boat.

The men disappeared to do their tasks. When they did, she turned to Hank, more pieces fitting together in her mind.

"You were paying off the former captain in order for him to look the other way while you use this vessel to transport drugs, weren't you?" Kenzie wasn't sure why she'd asked the question out loud, but maybe it would buy her some time or give her a better feel for what she was up against.

He shrugged as he glared at her. "What does it matter anymore?"

"Why did you kill him?"

The man turned away from her and began fiddling with the controls on the panel. "Bridgemore got greedy. Wanted more money. Threatened to turn us in. Even had some crazy cover story made up. I wasn't going to let that happen."

"So, what are you going to do with everyone onboard this boat?" Her heart thumped in her ears as she waited for what he had to say.

"With the new captain's criminal record, it should be easy to make him look incompetent. We'll make sure there's plenty of alcohol lying around so authorities will simply think he was irresponsible. I don't have all the details worked out yet, but that's the gist of it."

Kenzie glanced behind her and saw the SSAS—the Ship Security Alert System. If she could just reach the beacon . . . she could send an emergency message to the Coast Guard that they were in trouble.

She slowly took a small step closer. "You've got to know you won't get away with this."

He shrugged, brushing off her words. "Maybe not. But it will buy us some time."

"Are you the one who beat up Waldo?" She glanced at the button again. She still had two feet to go before she'd be close enough to hit it.

"He overheard Siv on the phone with me, so we had no choice but to silence him. We lured him off the boat, telling him that we had his mother held hostage and if he didn't come, we'd kill her. Then, of course, we set it up to make it look like Buster was the one responsible. Win-win!"

"It certainly sounds like you thought of everything."

"I'm good at what I do," Hank muttered. "What can I say?"

Kenzie would agree that he seemed confident in his plan of action. She hoped his arrogance would ultimately be his weakness.

If she could just get a little closer to that button . . .

Just then, Hank glanced over at her and sucked in a breath.

In two strides, he reached her and slapped his gun across her cheek. "I don't think so!"

As pain spread through her, Kenzie collapsed to the floor.

When she saw the hardened look in Hank's eyes, she knew it was too late to hit the button . . . and that she just might have ruined her chances of surviving also.

JIMMY JAMES PACED the small meeting room, trying to figure out what his next step should be.

One wrong move, and he was certain that someone could end up dead. That wouldn't be acceptable.

"We can't just sit here." Eddie leaned against the wall, sweat dotting his skin and an agitated look in his eyes.

"What do you propose that we do?" Jimmy James turned toward him, trying to ease the defensiveness from his voice.

"I don't know." Eddie threw his hands in the air. "But what if they try to kill us all?"

Nikki let out a cry behind him. "Do you think that's what they're going to do? Come back in here and just shoot us all dead?"

Jimmy James gave Eddie a pointed look. The last thing they needed was to get people panicking right now. Eddie seemed to realize his error, and he pressed his lips together before turning around as if he was trying to get a grip.

"Listen." Jimmy James turned to face the group, careful to keep his voice level. "Everyone just needs to keep a cool head until we can figure out what's happening here."

"Are you going to let us die in here?" Sylvia gripped her necklace as if it were a lifeline.

"I'm not going to let anybody die," Jimmy James said. "I just need time to think."

As soon as he said the words, he heard footsteps overhead.

People were quickly walking, almost as if they were in a hurry.

And the boat was moving again.

What in the world . . . ?

Siv must have known how to fix the engine —or maybe there had never really been anything wrong. Where were these guys taking his boat?

Jimmy James felt his muscles bristle. None of this was okay. And he had to stop them.

He began looking around the room, trying to find a way that they could get out of here. Or a way to send an SOS.

But there was nothing.

"What are you looking for?" Sylvia asked.

"Some way of communicating with the outside world," Jimmy James said. "Without our cell phones and radios, it's a little hard to do."

"Would this help?" Laney held up something in her hands.

It was one of the crew's radios.

"Where did you get that?" Sylvia asked.

Laney shrugged. "I swiped it off Eddie when he wasn't paying attention."

"What have I told you about taking things that don't belong to you?" Sylvia rushed.

That explained all the missing things on the boat —probably everything from his missing book to Kenzie's suitcase being gone through and possibly even her missing then magically reappearing earrings.

Jimmy James held out his hand. Right now, he wasn't complaining. "Why don't you two talk about that later? For now, this radio—and your daughter's stealing problem—is going to be an asset."

Sylvia scowled while Laney looked proud.

Just then, Jimmy James felt the boat changing course.

The bad feeling in his gut grew even deeper.

CHAPTER THIRTY-SEVEN

"WHAT ARE you going to do now?" Kenzie remained on the floor, her cheek throbbing. The man hulked over her, gun still in hand and a disgusted look on his face.

"I already told you. I'm going to run this boat aground. Get away with our loot. Leave you guys here with this boat as your casket."

She swallowed hard. He made it sound so simple, so normal.

But nothing about this was normal.

Kenzie's throat burned as she asked, "Why am I here and not in the room with everyone else?"

A gleam of malice sparked in the man's gaze. "Because sometimes it's good to have leverage."

The burn in her throat turned into an all-out ache. "I'm leverage?"

Kenzie didn't like the sound of that.

"Believe me, police won't be shooting if you're with us. Plus, you're kind of pretty, so you might come in handy." He smirked.

She wasn't sure what that meant, nor was she sure that she wanted to know.

"Why can't you just let us go? Take your cocaine and get your money for it. There's no reason to hurt innocent people."

"You've seen my face, for starters." He took a step back and shook his head.

"I wouldn't have if you hadn't taken your mask off. Why did you have to come onboard at all?" Something about his story still wasn't adding up completely.

"I tried to make things easy by coming aboard last night, but it didn't quite work out."

"Couldn't Siv have found what you were looking for?"

Hank narrowed his eyes in irritation. "Captain Bridgemore got greedy and moved our stash. Siv couldn't find it all, so I had to take matters into my own hands. Besides, we mostly wanted him onboard in case anything went wrong."

More puzzle pieces fell into place. "There has to be another way to resolve this besides hurting innocent people."

"Not really. Even more, we don't care. All we want is our payday."

Her stomach squeezed harder. How could they be this heartless? Would they leave any of them alive? She didn't know.

But she believed what this man had told her.

If they died, they would simply be collateral damage. All these guys cared about was getting the money from this drug deal.

JIMMY JAMES SENT the distress call via radio using Morse code. He hoped it worked.

Without help, they weren't going to get out of this situation alive.

But now he wanted another backup plan. He couldn't stand being in here while Kenzie was out there with those men.

He began examining the door. He'd already pushed against it, trying more than once to get it open. It hadn't worked.

But there had to be another way . . .

"What are you doing?" Eddie stepped closer.

"I need to find something hard, long, and narrow." Jimmy James continued to study the door.

"I don't understand."

Jimmy James touched the side of the door as he examined it. "I think I can remove these hinges and get out."

"How is that going to help us?" Eddie rushed. "They're just going to kill us!"

"We're not doing any good just sitting in here," Jimmy James said, undeterred by Eddie's feedback.

"If you open that door, we're all goners!" Buster joined in the conversation. His cheeks were flushed with an almost manic fear, and an air of panic surrounded him.

"Like Nikki said, who's to say they're not going to come back and kill us all if we stay in here?" Jimmy James locked his gaze with Buster's.

The two of them stared off for a minute. Buster was trying to figure out if he could trust Jimmy James. If he was their best bet.

Finally, he looked away and nodded with resignation. "What do you want to do when you get that door open?"

"I'm going to do everything in my power to stop these guys."

Nikki sat in the corner with her knees pulled to her chest and her red-rimmed eyes glaring with accusation. "By the time help gets here, they'll probably be long gone," she muttered. "And we could be dead."

Kenzie's image again filled his mind. If they stayed in here, *she* could be dead. He had to do everything in his power to keep her safe.

"Like I said earlier, we all need to keep a cool head here," Jimmy James said. "If there's anything that you can find that might serve as a weapon, grab it now."

Buster stepped in front of the door. "I can't let you do something that's going to put us all in danger."

"And I can't just sit here like a lame duck with these guys on our boat. The boat is moving right now. They're taking us somewhere away from our course."

"So?" Buster stared at him.

Jimmy James was going to have to spell everything out for him, it seemed. "The last thing we want is for them to take us out to the middle of the ocean and leave us there without any gas. Sitting in this room is not an option. I'll get out, and you guys can put the hinges back in and pretend like I'm still here if anybody comes back. But I'm getting out of this room."

Buster and Nikki both stared at him for a moment until finally nodding.

"Fine," Buster agreed. "We'll put the hinges back on the door."

Jimmy James nodded. "Good. Now, find something to help me take these hinges out."

He prayed that the Coast Guard was on its way.

If there was one thing Jimmy James was good at, it was fighting. Hand-to-hand combat had been a way of life at one point.

He just never thought those skills would come in handy again.

CHAPTER THIRTY-EIGHT

KENZIE COULDN'T SHAKE the panic bubbling inside her. She wished she could think of a way out of this. But she couldn't.

There was no way she could take on Hank, especially since he had a gun *and* his henchmen weren't far away.

Did these guys really plan on taking her with them? What would that mean?

She shivered. She didn't want to know.

Before Kenzie had a chance to dwell on the what ifs, the door to the bridge burst open, and the other two gunmen and Siv appeared.

"You'll never believe this, but we found the rest of the stash," Siv said.

Hank sucked in a breath. "Perfect. Where was it?"

"In the anchor compartment. That's where I suspected it might be, but I didn't have a chance to check until now. Too many people were always around."

"Brilliant," Hank muttered.

"We can get out of here now. We have some buyers who are very anxious for our delivery."

Hank smiled. "Perfect timing."

As he said the words, Kenzie heard something brush against the bottom of the boat before it lurched to a stop.

Hank had run them aground on that sandbar, hadn't he? Just like he said he was going to do.

More alarm flooded through her.

Hank stepped forward and grabbed Kenzie's arm again, squeezing it so hard she was sure it would bruise.

"Let's go," he muttered.

"You're taking her with us?" Siv stared at them, confusion stretching across his features.

"It's like I was just explaining to the steward—she's leverage. And leverage can be everything in situations like these."

"Or she could get in the way," Siv said.

"If she gets in the way, we get rid of her," Hank said. "I'm good with either of those. But for now, let's get moving."

"What about our hostages?"

Hank tugged Kenzie from the bridge, headed toward the deck. "I smashed the main radio and took the navigation chip out. No one's going to be able to find them for a while. Best-case scenario, we'll make them sweat. Worst-case scenario: they can all die down there together."

Kenzie's heart continued to pound into her ears.

That would be a cruel way to die.

But how could she help them—especially since she couldn't even help herself?

JIMMY JAMES STOOD behind the corner by the bridge and listened to everything that was being said on the deck only a few feet away.

There was no way that he could let them leave with Kenzie. He'd never see her again if that was the case.

He glanced around, trying to formulate a plan. But he didn't have long to think.

At once, he knew what he needed to do.

It was risky, but it was the only option that he had right now.

He drew in a deep breath and prayed for God's mercy before he acted.

The next instant, he charged from where he stood and tackled Hank.

The men had practically lined up like bowling pins. When he took Hank down, he knocked the other three down as well.

Jimmy James kept one hand on Hank's gun, knowing he had to keep the barrel aimed away from anyone.

The good news was, he was at least sixty pounds heavier than this guy and stronger too.

"I don't know what you think you're doing," Hank muttered.

Jimmy James glanced up at Kenzie long enough to see her standing there in horror.

"Run!" he told her.

She remained frozen another moment before finally sprinting away from the scene.

The moment of distraction allowed Hank to get the upper hand. He grabbed the gun and smacked it across Jimmy James' face. Pain rippled through his cheekbone.

The next instant, the gun was aimed at Jimmy James, and all four men surrounded him.

He'd been in fights before. But this one was stacked against him. He was outnumbered and out-weaponed.

He fisted his hands as the men circled him.

If this was purely a fist fight, he might be able to take them out.

But the guns changed everything.

"You shouldn't have done that," Hank muttered.

"I don't think you're in any position to lecture me," Jimmy James muttered. "Especially about what I should or should not be doing."

"Some people say, work harder," Hank added. "I say, work smarter."

Jimmy James glanced around at each of the men, wondering how he could take them all out.

But since all of them had their attention on him, it would be nearly impossible.

"While I take care of him, you find the girl," Hank ordered the man he'd called Lewy. "We've got to get off this boat before we have any more trouble."

Lewy scrambled away.

As he did, Hank raised his gun, about to fire.

When Jimmy James saw the other men with

their guns raised, he knew there was no need to fight.

He might be able to take out one gun, but there were two others still aimed at him.

And that put him in a very difficult position.

CHAPTER THIRTY-NINE

KENZIE COULDN'T WALK AWAY and let Jimmy James fight the battle for her.

His actions were noble, but this wasn't the way this was going to end. Not if she had a choice in the matter.

She hurried down the hallway, searching for something—anything—to use as a weapon.

Her gaze stopped on a fire extinguisher on the wall.

That would work.

She ducked low as she headed in the direction of the men. Quietly, she moved close enough to hear, "While I take care of him, you find the girl."

Adrenaline surged through her blood. He was talking about taking care of Jimmy James . . .

As she peeked around the corner, she saw the gun pointed at Jimmy James' chest, and all her fears were confirmed.

If she wanted to act, it had to be now.

Finding her courage, she jumped into the doorway, still gripping the fire extinguisher. Before the men could realize what was happening, she squeezed the handle and foam covered their faces.

They yelped with pain.

The foam would blur their vision—for a few seconds at least.

With the men distracted, Jimmy James grabbed Hank's gun and twisted it from his grip.

Jimmy James turned and pressed the weapon into her free hand. "Take this!"

Kenzie gasped as she stared at it. As she felt its weight. As she realized the responsibility of handling a gun.

She swallowed hard before raising the weapon, her hand on the trigger.

Jimmy James' fist hit the second-in-command in the face. The man stumbled backward before toppling over the railing and into the water.

As Siv's vision started to clear, Kenzie quickly shoved the gun into her waistband. She grabbed the fire extinguisher with both hands and pointed the nozzle. Spray hit his face again.

He yelled and fell to his knees.

She turned in time to see Jimmy James and Hank face off, fists in the air and snarls on their faces.

"You should have never boarded my boat." Jimmy James' razor-like gaze cut into Hank's.

"You should have never gotten involved with this," Hank barked back.

At once, Jimmy James charged toward the man. His shoulder met Hank's abdomen, and he knocked Hank to the deck.

As the two wrestled, Kenzie glanced back at Siv. With the foam wiped from his eyes, he started to reach for another gun—one she hadn't seen in the confusion.

Before he could grab it, she took the fire extinguisher and slammed it into his head.

He sank to the floor.

When she looked back up, she saw that Jimmy James had put Hank into a headlock.

She released the breath she held in and lowered the fire extinguisher. The man wasn't going anywhere —not with Jimmy James subduing him like that.

Could this all really be over?

As if to answer her question, she heard the roar of a motor outside. Heard footsteps boarding the boat.

The next instant, the Coast Guard announced themselves and surrounded them.

Lewy appeared from the salon, his hands in the air.

Help was here.

She and Jimmy James exchanged a glance.

Maybe this was all finally over.

AN HOUR LATER, the crew stood on the aft deck, each of them trying to process what had just happened.

The good news was that they were all alive— shaken but still living.

They were still out in the middle of the Atlantic. The Coast Guard had swarmed the boat. Hank and his henchmen had been arrested and the cocaine retrieved.

But there was still a lot more to process.

Plus, a tugboat had been sent to free them from the sandbar. Officials didn't believe there was any damage to the boat's hull, other than the fact that it was grounded.

As Jimmy James stared at Kenzie, who leaned against the wall, he fought the urge to move closer and put an arm around her shoulders. To tell her how impressed he was. How much she'd come to mean to him.

But it was too soon. Too public.

"I don't know about you all, but I'm just glad this is all over," Kenzie muttered.

"We all are." Jimmy James squared his shoulders as he addressed the group around him. "Crew, all things considered, I think we handled ourselves the best we could."

Eddie turned to Jimmy James and Kenzie, an apologetic frown on his face. "I just want to say I'm sorry. I wrote you both off because you were outsiders. I shouldn't have done that. You two saved us tonight."

Jimmy James glanced at Kenzie and shrugged. "You can thank Kenzie for that."

"If anything, it was a team effort," Kenzie said. "I'm just thankful it all turned out okay."

Sunni cleared her throat before saying, "Me too. Like I said earlier, I'm also sorry that I was hard on you. It was wrong of me."

"What's this mean for the future charters?" Durango asked. "No more six-course meals onboard for a while?"

"That will be up to Mr. Robertson—and possibly law enforcement." Jimmy James rubbed his jaw and shrugged.

Jimmy James glanced behind them into the main salon area where the Coast Guard questioned Buster and his family. It didn't appear any of them knew anything about what had happened. They were just as much victims as anyone else.

But Jimmy James could hardly wait to get off this boat. He could use some breathing room to sort out his thoughts—and the possibilities for his future.

This had certainly been an experience . . . possibly one that came once in a lifetime.

He could only hope, at least.

CHAPTER FORTY

BACK IN LANTERN BEACH, Kenzie felt a surprising bond with Buster and his bunch—so much so that she almost felt sad to tell them good-bye. The experience—and trauma—had brought them all together, at least for a moment.

Everyone hugged at the docks, and Kenzie was certain they'd never forget what had happened aboard *Almost Paradise*.

The boat had been freed from the sandbar with no damage and was now docked in the harbor at Lantern Beach. Mechanics were working to make sure no other destruction had been done to the vessel.

What a trip.

As soon as Buster was gone, the crew turned to each other.

"I guess we'll wait and see what Mr. Robertson says." Eddie pushed his sunglasses up higher on his nose. "In the meantime, we can hang out in Lantern Beach for a couple of days until we know what's going on."

"That's probably a smart idea," Jimmy James said. "Do you guys have a place to stay?"

"I'm hoping we can find some space at the campground," Eddie said. "The digs there were pretty sweet."

"If you can't, let me know. I'll see what I can do to help you out. I do have some connections in the area."

"We appreciate that." Eddie extended his hand. "Thanks again for everything you did."

Another round of hugs and handshakes went around before the rest of the crew disappeared, heading back to their cars.

But Kenzie lingered close to Jimmy James, anxious for a moment with him. They hadn't had a chance to talk since everything happened.

She stared up at him for a moment, unsure if she could find adequate words for this situation.

That's when she realized she couldn't.

Instead, she threw her arms around his shoulders and pulled him into a hug.

He let out a deep chuckle as he pulled her closer. "What's this for?"

"I'm just so grateful that you were with me on this charter. I might not be alive right now if you weren't. Thank you for everything."

"It was my pleasure," he murmured in her ear. "I'm glad that I could be there for you."

Hesitantly, she released her grip from his shoulders and stepped back. So many questions lingered in her mind, along with an uncertainty about what her future would look like—especially if Jimmy James wasn't a part of it.

"What's next for you?" she finally asked.

He shrugged and stared at the boats on the dock. "Apparently, I won't be captaining this next charter. Mr. Robertson has made that clear."

She frowned, even though she wasn't surprised. "I'm sorry to hear that. I know that establishing your career in the charter boat industry is important."

"There *is* good news." Jimmy James raised his eyebrows.

Her heart skipped a beat as she wondered what he was talking about. "What's that?"

He stepped closer, his eyes filling with warmth. "It means I'm no longer your captain."

A slow grin spread over her face. "I guess that is what it means, now, isn't it?"

Their gazes met. Part of her wanted to stand on her tiptoes and plant a kiss on his lips.

But another part of her reminded herself to take things slowly. There was no harm in doing that, but there *could* be a lot of harm in rushing a relationship.

Jimmy James shifted in front of her, swallowing so hard his Adam's apple bobbed up and down. "Look, I need to drop some things off at my place and get cleaned up. But how would you feel about going out for some ice cream tonight? I know a really great place."

Her grin widened at his invitation. "I would like that."

He shifted again. "Will you be staying at the campground with the rest of the crew?"

"I'm hoping to find a room at the inn. I could use a little break from them."

"I can't blame you. How about if I follow you there? If it's full, I happen to know someone who runs a retreat center. You can probably use one of those rooms tonight."

"Intriguing."

"It's actually the police chief."

She tilted her head. "You're just a mystery. You keep me guessing, Jimmy James."

"Anything you want to know, you can ask me. Maybe over that ice cream we were talking about?"

She reached forward and squeezed his thick hand. "That sounds wonderful."

A smile stretched across his face. "I'll see you in a few, Kenzie Anderson."

"I look forward to it, Captain Gamble."

He walked with her back to her car, and as he did, her pulse continued to race.

Kenzie was looking forward to having ice cream with Jimmy James more than she ever expected.

Could blue skies be ahead? She hoped so.

~~~

Thank you for reading *Run Aground*. If you enjoyed this book, would you please consider leaving a review?

COMING NEXT: DECK RECKONING

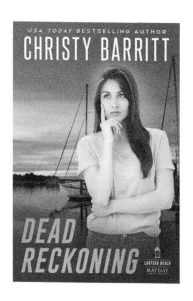

ALSO BY CHRISTY BARRITT:

You can take the detective out of the investigation, but you can't take the investigator out of the detective. A notorious gang puts a bounty on Detective Cady Matthews's head after she takes down their leader, leaving her no choice but to hide until she can testify at trial. But her temporary home across the country on a remote North Carolina island isn't as peaceful as she initially thinks. Living under the new identity of Cassidy Livingston, she struggles to keep her investigative skills tucked away, especially after a body washes ashore. When local police bungle the murder investigation, she can't resist stepping in. But

Cassidy is supposed to be keeping a low profile. One wrong move could lead to both her discovery and her demise. Can she bring justice to the island . . . or will the hidden currents surrounding her pull her under for good?

Flood Watch

The tide is high, and so is the danger on Lantern Beach. Still in hiding after infiltrating a dangerous gang, Cassidy Livingston just has to make it a few more months before she can testify at trial and resume her old life. But trouble keeps finding her, and Cassidy is pulled into a local investigation after a man mysteriously disappears from the island she now calls home. A recurring nightmare from her time undercover only muddies things, as does a visit from the parents of her handsome ex-Navy SEAL neighbor. When a friend's life is threatened, Cassidy must make choices that put her on the verge of blowing her cover. With a flood watch on her emotions and her life in a tangle, will Cassidy find the truth? Or will her past finally drown her?

Storm Surge

A storm is brewing hundreds of miles away, but its effects are devastating even from afar. Laid-back, loose, and light: that's Cassidy Livingston's new motto. But when a makeshift boat with a bloody cloth inside washes ashore near her oceanfront home, her detective instincts shift into gear . . . again. Seeking clues isn't the only thing on her mind—romance is heating up with next-door neighbor and former Navy SEAL Ty Chambers as well. Her heart wants the love and stability she's longed for her entire life. But her hidden identity only leads to a tidal wave of turbulence. As more answers emerge about the boat, the danger around her rises, creating a treacherous swell that threatens to reveal her past. Can Cassidy mind her own business, or will the storm surge of violence and corruption that has washed ashore on Lantern Beach leave her life in wreckage?

Dangerous Waters

Danger lurks on the horizon, leaving only two choices: find shelter or flee. Cassidy Livingston's new identity has begun to feel as comfortable as her favorite sweater. She's been tucked away on Lantern Beach for weeks, waiting to testify against a deadly gang, and is settling in to a new life she wants to last forever. When she thinks she spots someone malevolent from her past, panic swells inside her. If an enemy has found her, Cassidy won't be the only one who's a target. Everyone she's come to love will also be at risk. Dangerous waters threaten to pull her into an overpowering chasm she may never escape. Can Cassidy survive what lies ahead? Or has the tide fatally turned against her?

Perilous Riptide

Just when the current seems safer, an unseen danger emerges and threatens to destroy everything. When Cassidy Livingston finds a journal hidden deep in the recesses of her ice cream truck, her curiosity kicks into high gear. Islanders suspect that Elsa, the journal's owner, didn't die accidentally. Her final entry indicates their suspicions might be correct and that what Elsa observed on her final night may have led to her demise. Against the advice of Ty Chambers, her former Navy SEAL boyfriend, Cassidy taps into her detective skills and hunts for answers. But her search only leads to a skeletal body and trouble for both of them. As helplessness threatens to drown her, Cassidy is desperate to turn back time. Can Cassidy find what she needs to navigate the perilous situation? Or will the riptide surrounding her threaten everyone and everything Cassidy loves?

Deadly Undertow

The current's fatal pull is powerful, but so is one detective's will to live. When someone from Cassidy Livingston's past shows up on Lantern Beach and warns her of impending peril, opposing currents collide, threatening to drag her under. Running would be easy. But leaving would break her heart. Cassidy must decipher between the truth and lies, between reality and deception. Even more importantly, she must decide whom to trust and whom to fear. Her life depends on it. As danger rises and answers surface, everything Cassidy thought she knew is tested. In order to survive, Cassidy must take drastic measures and end the battle against the ruthless gang DH-7 once and for all. But if her final mission fails, the consequences will be as deadly as the raging undertow.

LANTERN BEACH ROMANTIC SUSPENSE

Tides of Deception

Change has come to Lantern Beach: a new police chief, a new season, and . . . a new romance? Austin Brooks has loved Skye Lavinia from the moment they met, but the walls she keeps around her seem impenetrable. Skye knows Austin is the best thing to ever happen to her. Yet she also knows that if he learns the truth about her past, he'd be a fool not to run. A chance encounter brings secrets bubbling to the surface, and danger soon follows. Are the life-threatening events plaguing them really accidents . . . or is someone trying to send a deadly message? With the tides on Lantern Beach come deception and lies. One question remains—who will be swept away as the water shifts? And will it bring the end for Austin and Skye, or merely the beginning?

Shadow of Intrigue

For her entire life, Lisa Garth has felt like a supporting character in the drama of life. The designation never bothered her—until now. Lantern Beach, where she's settled and runs a popular restaurant, has boarded up for the season. The slower pace leaves her with too much time alone. Braden Dillinger came to Lantern Beach to try to heal. The former Special Forces officer returned from battle with invisible scars and diminished hope. But his recovery is hampered by the fact that an unknown enemy is trying to kill him. From the moment Lisa and Braden meet, danger ignites around them, and both are drawn into a web of intrigue that turns their lives upside down. As shadows creep in, will Lisa and Braden be able to shine a light on the peril around them? Or will the encroaching darkness turn their worst nightmares into reality?

Storm of Doubt

A pastor who's lost faith in God. A romance writer who's lost faith in love. A faceless man with a deadly obsession. Nothing has felt right in Pastor Jack Wilson's world since his wife died two years ago. He hoped coming to Lantern Beach might help soothe the ragged edges of his soul. Instead, he feels more alone than ever. Novelist Juliette Grace came to the island to hide away. Though her professional life has never been better, her personal life has imploded. Her husband left her and a stalker's threats have grown more and more dangerous. When Jack saves Juliette from an attack, he sees the terror in her gaze and knows he must protect her. But when danger strikes again, will Jack be able to keep her safe? Or will the approaching storm prove too strong to withstand?

Winds of Danger

Wes O'Neill is perfectly content to hang with his friends and enjoy island life on Lantern Beach.

Something begins to change inside him when Paige Henderson sweeps into his life. But the beautiful newcomer is hiding painful secrets beneath her cheerful facade. Police dispatcher Paige Henderson came to Lantern Beach riddled with guilt and uncertainties after the fallout of a bad relationship. When she meets Wes, she begins to open up to the possibility of love again. But there's something Wes isn't telling her—something that could change everything. As the winds shift, doubts seep into Paige's mind. Can Paige and Wes trust each other, even as the currents work against them? Or is trouble from the past too much to overcome?

Rains of Remorse

A stranger invades her home, leaving Rebecca Jarvis terrified. Above all, she must protect the baby growing inside her. Since her estranged husband died suspiciously six months earlier, Rebecca has been determined to depend on no one but herself. Her chivalrous new neighbor appears to be an answer to prayer. But who is Levi Stoneman really? Rebecca wants to believe he can help her, but she can't ignore her instincts. As danger closes in, both Rebecca and Levi must figure out whom they can trust. With Rebecca's baby coming soon, there's no time to waste. Can the truth prevail . . . or will remorse overpower the best of intentions?

Torrents of Fear

The woman lingering in the crowd can't be Allison . . . can she? Because Allison was pronounced dead six years ago. Musician Carter Denver knows only one person who's capable of helping him find answers: Sadie Thompson, his estranged best friend and someone who also knew Allison. He needs to know if he's losing his mind or if Allison could have survived her car accident. Could Allison really be alive? If so, why is she trying to harm Carter and Sadie? As the two try to find answers, can Sadie keep her feelings for Carter hidden? Could he ever care for her, or is the man of her dreams still in love with the woman now causing his nightmares?

LANTERN BEACH PD

On the Lookout

When Cassidy Chambers accepted the job as police chief on Lantern Beach, she knew the island had its secrets. But a suspicious death with potentially far-reaching implications will test all her skills

—and threaten to reveal her true identity. Cassidy enlists the help of her husband, former Navy SEAL Ty Chambers. As they dig for answers, both uncover parts of their pasts that are best left buried. Not everything is as it seems, and they must figure out if their John Doe is connected to the secretive group that has moved onto the island. As facts materialize, danger on the island grows. Can Cassidy and Ty discover the truth about the shadowy crimes in their cozy community? Or has darkness permanently invaded their beloved Lantern Beach?

Attempt to Locate

A fun girls' night out turns into a nightmare when armed robbers barge into the store where Cassidy and her friends are shopping. As the situation escalates and the men escape, a massive manhunt launches on Lantern Beach to apprehend the dangerous trio. In the midst of the chaos, a potential foe asks for Cassidy's help. He needs to find his sister who fled from the secretive Gilead's Cove community on the island. But the more Cassidy learns about the seemingly untouchable group, the more her unease grows. The pressure to solve both cases continues to mount. But as the gravity of the situation rises, so does the danger. Cassidy is determined to protect the island and break up the cult . . . but doing so might cost her everything.

First Degree Murder

Police Chief Cassidy Chambers longs for a break from the recent crimes plaguing Lantern Beach. She simply wants to enjoy her friends' upcoming wedding, to prepare for the busy tourist season about to slam the island, and to gather all the dirt she can on the suspicious community that's invaded the town. But trouble explodes on the island, sending residents—including Cassidy—into a squall of uneasiness. Cassidy may have more than one enemy plotting her demise, and the collateral damage seems unthinkable. As the temperature rises, so does the pressure to find answers. Someone is determined that Lantern Beach would be better off without their new police chief. And for Cassidy, one wrong move could mean certain death.

Dead on Arrival

With a highly charged local election consuming the community, Police Chief Cassidy Chambers braces herself for a challenging day of breaking up petty conflicts and tamping down high emotions. But when widespread food poisoning spreads among potential voters across the island, Cassidy smells something rotten in the air. As Cassidy examines every possibility to uncover what's going on, local enigma Anthony Gilead again comes on her radar. The man is running for mayor and his cult-like following is growing at an alarming rate. Cassidy feels certain he has a spy embedded in her inner circle. The problem is that her pool of suspects gets deeper every day. Can Cassidy get to the bottom of what's eating away at her peaceful island home? Will voters turn out despite the outbreak of illness plaguing their tranquil town? And the even bigger question: Has darkness come to stay on Lantern Beach?

Plan of Action

A missing Navy SEAL. Danger at the boiling point. The ultimate showdown. When Police Chief Cassidy Chambers' husband, Ty, disappears, her world is turned upside down. His truck is discovered with blood inside, crashed in a ditch on Lantern Beach, but he's nowhere to be found. As they launch a manhunt to find him, Cassidy discovers that someone on the island has a deadly obsession with Ty. Meanwhile, Gilead's Cove seems to be imploding. As danger heightens, federal law enforcement officials are called in. The cult's growing threat could lead to the pinnacle standoff of good versus evil. A clear plan of action is needed or the results will be devastating. Will Cassidy find Ty in time, or will she face a gut-wrenching loss? Will Anthony Gilead finally be unmasked for who he really is and be brought to justice? Hundreds of innocent lives are at stake . . . and not everyone will come out alive.

LANTERN BEACH BLACKOUT

Dark Water

Colton Locke can't forget the black op that went terribly wrong. Desperate for a new start, he moves to Lantern Beach, North Carolina, and forms Blackout, a private security firm. Despite his hero status, he can't erase the mistakes he's made. For the past year, Elise Oliver hasn't been able to shake the feeling that there's more to her husband's death than she was told. When she finds a hidden box of his personal possessions, more questions—and suspicions—arise. The only person she trusts to help her is her husband's best friend, Colton Locke. Someone wants Elise dead. Is it because she knows too much? Or is it to keep her from finding the truth? The Blackout team must uncover dark secrets hiding beneath seemingly still waters. But those very secrets might just tear the team apart.

Safe Harbor

Guilt over past mistakes haunts former Navy SEAL Dez Rodriguez. When he's asked to guard a pop star during a music festival on Lantern Beach, he's all set for what he hopes is a breezy assignment. Bree hasn't found fame to be nearly as fulfilling as she dreamed. Instead, she's more like a carefully crafted character living out a pre-scripted story. When a stalker's threats become deadly, her life—and career—are turned upside down. From the start, Bree sees her temporary bodyguard as a player, and Dez sees Bree as a spoiled rich girl. But when they're thrown together in a fight for survival, both must learn to trust. Can Dez protect Bree—and his carefully guarded heart? Or will their safe harbor ultimately become their death trap?

Ripple Effect

Griff McIntyre never expected his ex-wife and three-year-old daughter to come to Lantern Beach. After an abduction attempt, they're desperate for safety. Now Griff's not letting either of them out of his sight. Bethany knows Griff is the only one who can protect them, despite the fact that he broke her heart. But she'll do anything to keep her daughter safe—even if it means playing nicely with a man she can't stand. As peril ripples through their lives, Griff and Bethany must work together to protect their daughter. But an unseen enemy wants something from them . . . and will stop at nothing to get it. When disaster strikes, can Griff keep his family safe? Or will past mistakes bring the ultimate failure?

Rising Tide

Benjamin James knows there's a traitor within his former command. The rest of his team might even think it's him. As danger closes in, he must clear himself and stop a deadly plot by a dangerous terrorist group. All CJ Compton wanted was a new start after her career ended under suspicion. Working as the house manager for private security group Blackout seems perfect. But there's more trouble here than what she left behind. As the tide rushes in, the stakes continue to rise. If the Blackout team fails, it's not just Lantern Beach at stake—it's the whole country. Can Benjamin and CJ overcome their differences and work together to find the truth?

LANTERN BEACH BLACKOUT: THE NEW RECRUITS

Rocco

Former Navy SEAL and new Blackout recruit Rocco Foster is on a simple in and out mission. But the operation turns complicated when an unsuspecting woman wanders into the line of fire. Peyton Ellison's life mission is to sprinkle happiness on those around her. When a cupcake delivery turns into a fight for survival, she must trust her rescuer— a handsome stranger—to keep her safe. Rocco is determined to figure out why someone is targeting Peyton. First, he must keep the intriguing woman safe and earn her trust. But threats continue to pummel them as incriminating evidence emerges and pits them against each other. With time running out, the two must set aside both their growing attraction and their doubts about each other in order to work together. But the perilous facts they discover leave them wondering what exactly the truth is . . . and if the truth can be trusted.

Axel

Women are missing. Private security firm Blackout must find them before another victim disappears. Axel

Hendrix likes to live on the edge. That's why being a Navy SEAL suited him so well. But after his last mission, he cut his losses and joined Blackout instead. His team's latest case involves an undercover investigation on Lantern Beach. Olivia Rollins came to the island to escape her problems—and danger. When trouble from her past shows up in town, she impulsively blurts she's engaged to Axel, the womanizing man she's seen while waitressing. Now, she may not be the only one in danger. So could Axel. Axel knows Olivia might be his chance to find answers and that acting like her fiancé is the perfect cover for his latest assignment. But he doesn't like throwing Olivia into the middle of such a dangerous situation. Nor is he comfortable with the feelings she stirs inside him. With Olivia's life—as well as both their hearts—on the line, Axel must uncover the truth and stop an evil plan before more lives are destroyed.

Beckett

When the daughter of a federal judge is abducted, private security firm Blackout must find her. Psychologist Samantha Reynolds doesn't know why someone is targeting her. Even after a risky mission to save her, danger still lingers. She's determined to use her insights into the human mind to help decode the deadly clues being left in the wake of her rescue. Former Navy SEAL Beckett Jones needs to figure out who's responsible for the crimes hounding Sami. He's not sure why he's so protective of the woman he rescued, but he'll do anything to keep her safe— even if it means risking his heart. As the body count rises, there's no room for error. Beckett and Sami must both tear down the careful walls they've built around themselves in order to survive. If they don't figure out who's responsible, the madman will continue his death spree . . . and one of them might be next.

Gabe

When former Navy SEAL and current Blackout operative Gabe Michaels is almost killed in a hit-and-run, the aftermath completely upends his life. He's no longer safe—and he's not the only one. Dr. Autumn Spenser came to Lantern Beach to start fresh. But while treating Gabe after his accident, she senses there's more to what happened to him than meets the eye. When she digs deeper into his past, she never expects to be drawn into a deadly dilemma. Gabe has been infatuated with the pretty doctor since the day they met. Now, can he keep her from harm? Could someone out of his league ever return his feelings or will her past hurts keep them apart? As danger continues to pummel them, Gabe and Autumn are thrown together in a quest to find answers. More important than their growing attraction, they must stay alive long enough to stop the person desperate to destroy them.

ABOUT THE AUTHOR

USA Today has called Christy Barritt's books "scary, funny, passionate, and quirky."

Christy writes both mystery and romantic suspense novels that are clean with underlying messages of faith. Her books have won the Daphne du Maurier Award for Excellence in Suspense and Mystery, have been twice nominated for the Romantic Times Reviewers' Choice Award, and have finaled for both a Carol Award and Foreword Magazine's Book of the Year.

She is married to her Prince Charming, a man who thinks she's hilarious—but only when she's not trying to be. Christy is a self-proclaimed klutz, an avid music lover who's known for spontaneously bursting into song, and a road trip aficionado.

When she's not working or spending time with her family, she enjoys singing, playing the guitar, and exploring small, unsuspecting towns where people have no idea how accident-prone she is.

Find Christy online at:
www.christybarritt.com
www.facebook.com/christybarritt
www.twitter.com/cbarritt

Sign up for Christy's newsletter to get information on all of her latest releases here: **www.christybarritt.com/newsletter-sign-up/**

If you enjoyed this book, please consider leaving a review.

Made in the USA
Las Vegas, NV
17 October 2024

97046611R00194